Coming About
…Finding Life's Compass

Patricia Thompson

DEDICATION

I would like to dedicate this book to the town of Depoe Bay, Oregon. From the shopkeepers and the residents, that put up with us tourists. To the Coast Guard, that puts their life on the line every day, protecting the coastline and rescuing all those that become lost, injured or stranded.

"For I know the plans I have for you," declares the Lord, "plans to prosper you and not harm you, plans to give you hope and a future."
Jeremiah 29:11

ACKNOWLEDGMENTS

I want to thank Clary Grant, one of the owners of Gracie's Sea Hag Restaurant, for sharing her scrapbook about Gracie and the restaurant's history. It was a wealth of information.

I was able to gather more information about Gracie and her family from the book, *Amazing Gracie and the Sea Hag*, by: Thorn and Ursula Bacon.

With these resources, I was able to add a true account of Depoe Bay's legendary Gracie.

If Gracie were with us today, I would have liked to thank her for all her contributions that helped make Depoe Bay, Oregon a very special place. It is very dear to me, as it is to many others that have visited and fallen in love with its charm.

Gracie Strom (September 28, 1928 – February 28, 2015)

CHAPTER 1

The sun was trying to burn through the gray heavy clouds. Mathew was standing at the kitchen window, sipping his coffee. Looking out over the ocean. His house was built up the hill from the sea wall, just inside the small town of Depoe Bay, Oregon.

Mathew Jones was a tall slender man with a strong build. A sturdy man, with dark graying hair. Many years of hard work had left its mark on him. As a fisherman, he spent much of his time out on the open ocean, and it left his hands and face weathered.

Mathew and his wife Suzie had been discussing their child Gary, the evening before. Mathew was using the quiet of the early morning hours to mull over their conversation. Little Gary was their only child, introverted and shy. They were constantly worrying about him. He had been sickly most of his young childhood. To keep him as well as possible, they decided to keep him home and teach him themselves. Having had traditional schooling, Mathew and Suzie had many doubts about the way they were raising their child, and would stop to reevaluate their decision, often. Each time they found it to be the right decision.

Gary did remarkably well in his studies. He was a conscientious student and very bright. When his parents went through the evaluation process they would find he was above his grade level in most subjects, and had more recreation time than other children his age. The only thing they had difficulty addressing, concerned them very much. Gary was still stuck in his shell. He was personable and polite to the towns' people when he was with family, but if he were out by himself, he barely said anything to anyone. His only friend was his Grandfather.

One day Gary's Grandfather came over to visit. He was an old salty fisherman. Bill Jones was an elderly man, strong and sturdy. His wiry beard was gray, long and full. Jeans and a t-shirt or long sleeved thermal was his dress of choice. It was usually covered by a big yellow rain suit with a yellow hat, for the frequently rainy coastal weather.

When he wasn't wearing his coat you could see his wide sturdy suspenders holding up his blue jeans. Gary loved it when he heard the clump, clump, clump of his Grandfather's big black rain boots. Every time he saw him, Gary felt as though his Grandfather had just stepped out of another world. One of adventure. It was his normal everyday fishing attire, but to Gary it was the outfit of a traveler of the sea.

Gary's excitement was always bountiful when his Grandfather came over. Bill was a very special man full of love and admiration for his grandson. Their bond was strong from the day Gary was born.

On this particular day, Gary's Grandfather had a surprise for him. "Well, young man. How are you this fine day?"

"I'm great!" Gary said in his 'excited to see you' voice.

"We are going to start you on your sailor training, today. The first thing we need to do, is get you used to long voyages."

"What do you mean, Grandfather?"

"How would you like to go out on the boat with me and your father for an entire week of fishing?"

"Can I, really?!"

"Yes, of course you can. Today we pack and get our rigging together. Tomorrow we leave, bright and early."

Gary was overjoyed!

The whole day was a great learning experience. He learned how to pack a sea bag, and got to help with the shopping, for food and supplies. Then, in the afternoon, he helped pack the boat. That night he could hardly sleep. He was so excited!

In the morning he awoke very early. Gary got dressed, grabbed his sea bag and headed downstairs to breakfast. Seated at the breakfast table, he found his father in the middle of eggs, sausage, toast and coffee.

As his Mother handed him a plate full of food, she said. "Good morning. Are you ready to start your adventure?"

"Yes!" Gary said eyeing his plate.

"Your Grandfather should be here anytime now." Mathew said.

About ten minutes later the doorbell rang. Gary sprang out of his seat. Before his mom could stop him, he was at the front door.

Mathew walked up behind his son and greeted his Father. The three of them proceeded to the kitchen. Suzie had a hot plate of food and steaming cup of coffee waiting on the table for Bill.

After breakfast Gary, his Father and Grandfather gathered their belongings, and said their good-byes to Suzie.

Gary gave her a kiss. "Bye Mom. Don't worry. I'll be a good sailor."

"Bye dear. I love you." Mathew said, kissing his wife.

"You three have a great time. Bye."

Grandfather gave her a smile and a wave, as they walked out the door.

At the boat, Bill, showed Gary where to stow the gear. Soon they were casting off. It was a good day to start. The skies were clear and bright; the salt air was cool and crisp.

They sailed along about two or three hours before stopping to set anchor. The rest of the day was spent setting and retrieving nets. Gary was so tired that night, he barely touched his dinner. He even fell asleep before he was fully dressed for bed.

"What a big grown up guy. He worked so hard today." Mathew stated.

"He sure did. That boy did a great job! Kind of reminds me of you, on your first trip. You were trying so hard to please me." Bill said, with a smile.

The next morning was as salty, calm and clear as the day before. It was glorious, but as the day wore on, the skies slowly grew dark. Grandfather hollered, "Pull in the nets!"

Just as the last net was in, the rain began to fall. It gradually grew into a mighty storm. They quickly got the last of their gear stowed away as the winds began to howl. The wind and rain stormed for the next three days. It raged so hard they found it impossible to fish. Gary wasn't allowed on deck during the course of the storm. He was very frustrated and bored, but he knew he had to listen and do as he was told. It was to keep him safe. Gary did the best he could to help, but mostly stayed out of the way. He found himself scared. Something he wasn't expecting. Although, he did well, trying to hide it.

Mathew and Bill saw how he was keeping his fear to himself. They were so proud of Gary and wanted to help. Looking back to when they were boys, Mathew and Bill remembered how they would have felt if someone could have seen through them. They decided to not to let on.

When the storm finally passed, Gary was given his duties and allowed back on deck. Everything was a mess. It took most of the day to clean it up. When everything was just about finished, Grandfather nudged his grandson. "Why don't you try and catch us a fish dinner?"

Gary was ready to take a break. He grabbed his rod and reel, and happily threw his line out into the water. The next two hours rolled by. He caught enough fish for a grand dinner. It was the first fresh dinner in three days. Everyone was relieved the hardship was over, and a good hot meal was just what they needed. They were able to relax and enjoy their evening.

The rest of the trip was pretty uneventful. When they got home Gary was enthusiastically telling his mother all about his trip. He went on and on about the fishing and helping. Of course, he told her all about the storm. This worried Suzie. She was aware that there were storms and was prepared that they were part of fishing in the sea. Hearing her son describe it and the things he went through, caught her emotionally off guard. She thought she was prepared for his first extended boat trip. She wasn't. It was a good experience for everyone.

As time passed Gary spent more and more time on the boat. This became his favorite most comfortable place to be. One day Gary and his Grandfather were fishing off the boat. They were anchored just outside the harbor. It was a nice relaxing day. A day for chit-chat and just hanging out. Gary really enjoyed times like these. As he would grow, he would treasure them even more.

On this particular day the conversation drifted here and there. Somehow they started talking about storms and how things were in Grandfather's day.

"Did I ever tell you the story of Gracie and how she came to own The Sea Hag?" Grandfather, Bill Jones asked.

Gracie's Sea Hag was Gary's favorite restaurant. They went by there on the way home from the harbor. Most days, they would stop in. Bill usually just ordered a drink. Gary would sit and listen to Grandfather and the other sailors swap stories, while he sat eating their Famous Clam Chowder. If they were lucky, on special days, Gracie would play her whiskey bottles.

"I don't think I've heard the real story of Gracie's Sea Hag. Please tell me." Gary said enthusiastically. He loved when Grandfather told him stories, especially true stories about places he'd been.

"Dick and Gracie Strom came to Depoe Bay with their three small children, when it was still a small fishing village. It was even quieter then, than it is today. We only had about one hundred and fifty residents. Why they chose our town..." Grandfather's mind started drifting in a different direction, as it did sometimes when he was reminiscing. "I guess that's why there are residents and tourists. People come here and fall in love with the sea and our happy community. Others enjoy it, but their lives are lived elsewhere. Depoe Bay is just a break from the world."

Grandfather slowly gazed out to the horizon as he was transported to an earlier time in his life. He and his late wife, Sarah were very happy when they found Depoe Bay. After settling in, they grew to love it even more.

When Bill started thinking about old times, he couldn't help but think of Sarah. It was the only time Gary saw true sadness in his Grandfather's eyes. One time he even caught a couple of tears rolling down his face. Bill, being the man and caring grandfather that he was, made sure to impress upon Gary that crying was okay, even for a man. "Never be afraid to shed tears, son. Especially over something that touches your heart."

Gary never forgot the lesson.

"Grandfather, Grandfather?!" Gary said, pulling on his shirt sleeve.

Bill came back to reality. "I'm sorry. I was just thinking about your Grandmother."

"That's okay, but please finish the story?!" Gary asked, intently.

"Okay," Grandfather said with a smile. "Well, they bought the restaurant, which is now Gracie's Sea Hag. It was not then, what it is today. The Strom's made many improvements, and really turned it into something special. It is said that Dick Strom was great with the financial end of things and Gracie's warm sparkling personality, kept people coming in. The town was so small and undiscovered that she had to come up with different ideas to bring in costumers. My favorite is her ability to play the whiskey bottles. I love how she taps them in rhythm. Each one with its own sound. She sure knows some very delightful tunes."

"I know. She's great!" Gary stated. "What happened to her family?"

"Her husband passed away and her children are mostly grown. They all keep in close contact and help out, sometimes at the restaurant. You've met them, Nancy, Larry and Sally."

"Oh, I have met them. Doesn't Larry sell fish?"

"Yes, he does." Grandfather was happy to see he paid attention to things that happened around him. As Bill had seen before, his Grandson was much more aware of things than people realized.

CHAPTER 2

One day, while helping on the boat, Gary met a little girl named Alice. Her father was one of the fisherman that harbored his boat in Depoe Bay. Alice was an only child. She and her Father and Mother lived in town. During the winter, while attending school, she wasn't allowed to spend a lot of time on the docks. In past summers, she spent time with her father on his boat, but her time was limited to when he could keep an eye on her. Being nine years old, this was the first summer her parents felt she was old enough to look after herself, and stay out of trouble. So they decided, Alice could come and stay all day, to help out her father. It made her happy because the harbor was her favorite place to be.

She was smart like Gary, but much more outgoing. They found they had a lot in common. Alice liked to spend time on the sandy beach and in the tide pools looking for shells and crabs. Gary did too.

There was quite a bit of down time, for kids. Fishing boats required a lot of work, but many of the jobs were too difficult or dangerous for them. During their down time, Gary and Alice were happy to have found each other. They enjoyed spending their afternoons together.

Most days they were on the boats until lunch. Afterwards, they would hang out around the sea shore, until it was time to go home. They would collect sea shells and rocks, wade through tide pools or do a little fishing. Some days Gary would go home with pockets full of shells and rocks. He brought them home so often, he began a rock garden. It was decorated with many colored shells and of course rocks. Other days he came home with the fish he caught. Gary would clean and scale them. Then give them to his Mother, and she would happily cook them for dinner. This pleased him very much.

As time went by, Gary grew in size and confidence. His friendship with Alice was helping him. Mathew and Suzie began feeling some relief about their son's future. Although, he was becoming more social, most of the time, he still preferred to be alone.

Alice continued to be his only friend, and he seemed to be happy with things that way. Gary enjoyed time by himself. He loved to think. Some days he would sit by the ocean for hours. He was always thinking about the future, and how he would have his own boat. One of the things he thought about often was how he could expand his Father's business. He wanted to grow it into something that would make more money for him and his family, more than just enough to cover expenses.

The older Gary grew, the deeper, more mature his thoughts became. When he was about fifteen years old, Gary and Alice started to notice new feelings growing between them. They seemed to feel closer than just casual friends. They had become best friends, and over the next year their friendship would begin to grow into something deeper.

Just after his sixteenth birthday, Gary's life changed. It happened late one night. He had been working on the docks all day, preparing for a long fishing trip. Gary decided to sleep on the boat, and get an early start in the morning. It was a common thing for him. He had begun staying on the boat a lot. It gave him a chance to be alone and think. It also gave him time to prepare for the next morning's duties. As he settled into bed with his favorite book, Gary thought he had heard a noise. He listened intently for a moment. Dismissing it, he went back to his book. The boat's rocking on the waves, the birds' talking and all the other noises that comforted him, took over. Gary began to fall asleep. Just as he was dropping off...he definitely heard a noise! Then he heard footsteps on the deck of the boat. Thinking it was just his dad checking on him, Gary popped his head out the cabin door.

"Hey, dad..." He started to say.

But, he was interrupted. Someone knocked him on the head. A lot of time passed before Gary found himself waking with a pounding headache. It took him a while to come out his haze and realize what was happening. Soon as he could sit up, Gary struggled to figure out where he was. He closed his eyes. Listened. Felt. Smelled. Listening, he could hear sounds from the open waters. Gary felt the room swaying, the coolness of the sea breeze. He could smell sea water, boat fuel, grease, raw fish, food cooking and a variety of unidentifiable smells. With all the information cataloged in his brain, he opened his eyes. The room was dark and damp. He tried to stand, only to find, he was chained to the floor. Gary began to get scared.

After a couple of hours sitting, wondering what was going to happen next, he heard someone coming down a flight of stairs. Gary was anxious with anticipation and fear for what might come next. The lock turned and the door slowly opened. A light streamed in through the doorway, blinding him. The figure of a large man came through the door. Gary was grateful for the break from the blinding light, but it didn't ease his fears.

"Come on. It's time to meet your captain." The man's voice was gruff and stern. He unlocked Gary from the floor, being careful to keep the chains secured around his wrists.

"What is going on? Where am I? How far out to sea are we? Where…"

The man stopped Gary. "Be quiet. You ask the captain." He started pushing him around.

Rather than resist, he decided to go along quietly. He wanted to get the whole picture before figuring out what to do. Gary figured the weaker he showed he was to his captures, the better. He would be able to use it to his advantage, later.

The hallway was dark and cold. The man and Gary walked for a long time. All the doors were made of a heavy dark wood, secured with big metal latches. They finally came to the last one. As the man opened the door, a warm glow came out and greeted Gary. He was happy to feel the heat as he entered the room.

Sitting behind a large oak desk was a big burly sea captain. He was trying to intimidate Gary, but he wasn't impressed. Although, Gary did try to mask his feelings, and look intimidated.

"We have selected you to join our crew. You will travel with us to Mexico. Where you will join another crew," was all the captain had to say.

"Yes sir, Captain." Gary responded.

The Captain pointed to his chains. The sailor that brought Gary in, released him. He stood, waiting for instructions. Gary figured if he tried to escape now, he would fail. But if he waited, he could earn their trust, and they would let their guard down. Then it would be time to get away.

The sailor took Gary to his quarters. As he entered the room, he could see they were simple and clean. It was cold with a dampness hanging in the air. Gary wished for the heat of the captain's quarters, but at least there were blankets and company here. He shared the quarters with four other men. All of them, had been shanghaied too.

The next few weeks went by uneventfully. Gary did all that was expected of him. When night time came, he was exhausted. Although, not too exhausted, to come up with a plan of escape.

Gary got started on his plan right away, by getting to know his roommates. They told each other their stories. One man was Richard. He was about fifty, strong and sturdy. Oldest of all the roommates. Quiet and gruff, he had lots of wiry gray whiskers. He spent most of his life as a longshoreman. The day he was taken, Richard was at a bar outside Lincoln Beach, Oregon, celebrating his retirement. He was finally able to move near his family. They took him because of his strong back and extensive experience.

Another man, Adam, was eighteen. He visiting a bar in Manzanita, Oregon, celebrating his birthday. All of his friends left him when he became drunk, obnoxious and only wanted to fight. They were there with fake IDs, and this added to his friends' concerns about getting into trouble. After they took off, he became an easy target. His captors took him because he was young and strong.

During Adam's imprisonment he was always talking, asking questions, complaining, making a general nuisance of himself. Twice he tried to escape. Both times he was caught, beaten, thrown into a single cabin and locked up.

When he spoke to any of the other prisoners on the ship, he was usually talking about plans to escape. Adam spoke to Gary a lot. He couldn't understand why Gary didn't want to listen, but Gary knew this man was young and green. Gary, even though younger, saw how foolish Adam was, so he kept to himself.

The next roommate was Dillon. He was in his late twenties or early thirties and was taken for his strength. He was at a bar in Florence, Oregon. After weeks of little sleep and a very long day, he stopped in for a beer. Two guys came in, pretending to know him. They knocked him on the head in such a way that it looked like he just passed out. Then took him out of the bar. It was a good scam.

The fourth man was about the same age as Dillon. His name was Jessy. He was the typical sort of guy that was shanghaied. Jessy was in the bar every night, and never left it sober. He couldn't even remember where he was when they took him. Getting him was easy. They just waited outside.

Gary, Richard, Dillon and Jessy just kept to themselves and did their jobs. They didn't want problems. All four of them were grateful to Adam. He distracted their captors. They were so concerned about what Adam was doing, where he was, what he was up to, that they paid little attention to the rest of the men. At one point, their captors, even took Adam out of their little group. Having him work separately; under constant supervision. When it was time to quit he was immediately placed back in the single cabin and locked away until breakfast.

Late at night, when most of the boat was asleep, the four men would whisper. They made a plan. The last few hours, before they landed in Mexico, the guards would be worrying about Adam. The four of them would slip over the side and swim to shore. Knowing they would be close to shore, and their captors would be getting them ready to depart, the men figured they would all be chained together. So they practiced going through the motions of swimming as though they were all chained together. When the time came to go overboard, they weren't chained at all. Gary, Richard, Dillon and Jessy were amazed.

Adam had a plan of his own. He would wait until the last minute and rush the captain. Then take him hostage. When he implemented his plan, it was very unsuccessful for him, but served as just the distraction the other four men needed. As Adam was rushing the captain, Gary, Richard, Dillon and Jessy, just slipped over the side. Then simply swam away.

When the four men found they weren't chained, they made a last minute decision to go in different directions. Thus increasing their odds of success by four.

He found himself, alone, approaching a sandy beach. Knowing it would leave him exposed and easy to spot, Gary looked around at the coast line. As he was treading water, he saw an out cropping of rocks, so he diverted his course toward it. Gary reached the shore just north of the harbor, where the boat was to dock, now that they were in Mexico. In front of him was a cave. Upon further investigation, he found that it went all the way through to the back side of the hill. Seeing that it gave him an easy escape. Just in case they were still out there searching for him, and due to the fact he was rather tired from the swim, he decided to rest awhile.

About half an hour passed by. Gary decided to check out his surroundings. He went to the back of the cave and slowly crept out. Being very cautious, he determined no one was around. To the left was a long empty beach. Down the hill and to the right was the harbor. Gary moved to a position with a better view of the harbor, being sure to stay hidden behind the outcroppings of rocks.

He saw the ship he had just escaped from, docked. There wasn't much sign of life on deck, but the dock was buzzing with activity. Figuring his captors were too busy with their cargo, Gary decided to start his journey home now. He hoped that they were waiting until nightfall to search for the missing men. Then all the honest men would be at home or in bars and not concerned with someone's illegal activities.

By sunset, Gary was about ten miles away. He traveled toward the mountains, keeping away from towns where he might be spotted. When it was dark, he found himself by a stream. By this time, his clothes were dry from being in the hot sun, but he was tired and hungry. As he took a long thirst quenching drink, exhaustion took over and he fell asleep next to the stream.

He awoke to sound of rushing water and birds singing their morning melodies. Gary was surprised he had slept all night. The early morning sun was already warming his face. It was going to prove to be another hot day. He decided to follow the water farther upstream into the mountains.

Along the way he found the most delicious berries he had ever eaten. Gary found many varieties of nourishment, as he traveled on his way to freedom. There were berries, of course, and nuts, roots, even insects. Hungry as he was, Gary didn't care what he ate, as long as it was edible.

Midway through the day, he stumbled upon a cave. It wasn't as big as the one on the beach, but it was sufficient to give him shelter. He gathered some pine boughs and moss. With those things he was able to make a comfortable warm bed in the cave. It was a good place to spend a long time, so he decided to stay. He would hide out until enough time passed that he could go back to town, without being searched for.

Every day was like summer vacation, when he and his Father would go backpacking. There was plenty of fish, fresh water, berries, roots and other plants. Gary had fun spending his days making things that helped him with his survival. He fashioned a trap for fish out of twigs. Used a rock to make a sharp tool for cutting. For four days he was happy and comfortable, and Gary would have stayed longer, but he had to get on his way. He needed to get back to the nearest town. It was time to find a way to make it home to Oregon and his family.

Gary gathered the fish he had dried and some berries, in preparation for the next day. Waking early, he had to wait a short time for the sun to come up enough that he could see his way downstream. Soon as it was, he was on his way. He had forgotten how long he had walked to get there. It took him all day to get close to the harbor. Being late in the afternoon, he decided to stay in the woods outside town, until the next day. Gary wanted to make sure his captors had left the harbor before getting too close.

The berries and fish he had, had been gone since lunch, and he didn't find any more around where he was. Too tired to search out food, he went to sleep hungry. He was out before the sun went down. He tossed and turned all night long, waking up every few hours. Gary was nervous being close to the harbor. He hoped the sailors weren't looking for him anymore, but he wouldn't know 'til morning. It had been a long night. He was awakened by the light of the sun as it started to spread its rays across the sky.

Gary investigated the harbor, from a safe distance, and found the boat that brought him here to Mexico, was gone. It was a relief. He had waited long enough. Now it would be safe to go to the town, down the road from the harbor. It was a common habit for Gary to hide some money in his boot. Thankfully, he had repeated this habit in the afternoon before being shanghaied, late in the evening. Pulling it from his boot, Gary moved half of his money to his pocket and put the remainder back in his boot.

The road to the next town was difficult, especially on an empty stomach. He found a small café and decided to treat himself to a good meal. It was crowded with people from all walks of life. This put Gary at ease, a little. He felt less like an outsider. It was a normal stopping off point for some of the English speaking tourists, so many of the staff spoke broken English. This helped him feel better. Gary didn't speak any Spanish.

After breakfast, Gary began thinking of how he might get back into the United States. He had always heard not to trust the Mexican police. There were rumors, back in the States, that many of them were bought off. Gary was sure it was just talk, but then again he was in a foreign country, without much money or identification. Most likely, all he had heard was just talk, but Gary was afraid to take that chance.

He began wandering around carefully, trying not to be noticed. Gary saw a boy about eight or ten. He looked like he was wise for his age and knew his way around.

Gary walked up to him. "Hi. Do you speak English?"

The boy looked at him, acting puzzled.

Gary didn't know any Spanish. He felt stupid. Bowing his head in frustration, Gary turned and started to walk away.

"Hey!" The boy called after him.

Gary stopped and turned around.

"I speak ... little English. I am Pedro." The boy said, seeming to size Gary up as he spoke.

"My name is Gary." He wasn't sure at this point if he should tell Pedro anything.

"Come," Pedro said, "We should leave the street." He motioned for Gary to follow him. He ducked down a side street, and Gary followed. "It isn't safe for gringos, after dark." Pedro continued.

Gary was glad to find someone who knew their way around. He was very cautious about trusting Pedro, but he had decided to take a chance. Gary paused a moment, and Pedro directed him to continue to follow, smiling reassuringly. They walked down the side street and stopped at a door. It was painted bright yellow with green trim. It was a dramatic contrast to the gray drab walls of the building. "This my casa. Come inside." Pedro said, in his broken English.

Gary entered a small kitchen. As he walked all the way in the door, he saw the house was one big room. On one side was the kitchen. The along the opposite wall was a small couch. In the middle of the room, was a square table, with four unmatched chairs around it. Off to one side Gary observed two doors, one lead to the restroom, and the other seemed to be a closet. Once he was all the way inside, he was greeted by Pedro's mother. She spoke Spanish very quickly. Gary had little idea what she was saying, so he just smiled and shook her hand. Pedro said something back. His Mother smiled and brought them some beans and tortillas. It was a simple meal, but Gary felt like it was a feast. He was so hungry. After dinner he slept on their floor.

In the morning, Gary began telling Pedro about his misadventures. He wasn't sure how much he should tell Pedro, but decided to tell him everything. After a breakfast of beans, egg, tortillas and coffee, Gary and Pedro discussed ways that he might get back home. It was very complicated. They discussed, that being on the Pacific coast in Mexico, the closest US state was California. Neither Pedro, his Mother nor Gary had ever been to southern California, so no one knew what to expect. In the end, they decided Gary just needed to get back into America. Then he would have to figure out what to do next.

Pedro waited until it was dark. Then he and Gary traveled all night to a place where they could hide out during most of the day. This process went on for three days and on the fourth night they reached the Tijuana River. Pedro showed Gary a small row boat.

"If you row at night, hide during the day. You can reach a safe spot, go ashore." Pedro said. He showed Gary, on a map, where to stop and hide during the day. Then where to go ashore on the American side.

"What about your boat?" Gary knew there was no way to get it back to Pedro.

"Don't worry. It not my boat. It boat of

coyotes."

"What is a coyote?"

"They run people and drugs across boarder."

Gary's eyes grew wide. He was surprised and scared. "I can't take their boat. If they catch me...I don't know what they'll do."

"Don't worry. People do this all time." Pedro smiled and motioned for him to get into the boat.

Gary took a note pad and pencil out of his pocket. "Give me your address. We can keep in touch."

Pedro wasn't sure if he should. He wasn't very trusting either. Gary convinced him it would be fun to keep in contact, and assured him he would write when he was able. Then he gave Pedro his address in Oregon. They shook hands and said good-bye. Gary got into the row boat and set off to America.

It was scary. Gary didn't know if the coyotes really wouldn't mind him borrowing their boat, but he had to get back across the border. Without identification and money there really wasn't any other choice. He stuck to the plan and hid out during the day and rowed during the night.

After, about a week, Gary started seeing signs in English. As the sun came up the following day, he found he was back on the American side. He located the place where he was supposed to leave the boat. Then tied it up, and found his way to the road.

Gary's arms were very tired, and he was hungry, again. Pedro had given him some food, but it was gone. Since it was still early in the day, he decided to start walking. He walked and walked. It took a day and a half to get to the nearest town.

Gary happened upon a small country store with a help wanted sign posted. Thinking he would need identification and references, Gary almost passed it by. He figured it was worth a chance. If nothing else, maybe he could work long enough to earn a meal.

The store keeper and his wife were very nice, and could see Gary had, had a rough time of it, lately. They took pity in him. "Do you mind cleanin' up?" The store keeper asked.

"No, I can do anything you need."

It was a good job. They gave him a cot in the back and meals. The pay was small, but that didn't matter to Gary. He was grateful for whatever he could get. Two weeks passed, and the store keeper was able to find a full time employee, that was going to stay on permanently. It was a good time for Gary and the shop owners to part-company. He thanked them and said good-bye, happy to be on his way. They told him, he was always welcome and to come by, if he was ever out their way again.

This time he had enough money to get a bus to San Diego. Once in there, Gary felt much more at ease. He was able to find some temporary work on the docks. After a couple of days, he had enough money to get a room at a local inn.

His journey that started out so perilously, and not of his choosing, was turning into quite an adventure. Gary was thoroughly enjoying life.

As time went by, he was sure his family was worried. He decided to drop them a postcard. A call would have been better, but he was afraid they would talk him into coming home, and Gary was definitely not ready for that.

Back home, Gary's Mother and Father had barely slept since their son had disappeared. His

Father searched the nearby towns. Asked everyone if they had any information. They had called the police, and gotten all the departments, in the surrounding areas, involved. Gary's parents were pressing them. The FBI was contacted, but they treated the case as just another runaway.

The day the postcard came Suzie was in the kitchen preparing lunch for Mathew and Bill. Mathew checked the mailbox on the way into the house. He let out a hoot and a holler!

"Suzie…Suzie! Our boy is okay."

She was beside herself in shock. Suzie found herself sitting in a chair. Not knowing what to think.

"How…where is he?"

"Here, read this." Mathew said, handing Suzie the postcard.

She was so happy. Tears were streaming down her face and made it impossible to read anything. Mathew gently took back the card and read it to her:

Hi, Mom and Dad.

I just wanted to let you know I'm fine. I'm

working odd jobs to earn enough money to get back home. I will write more, later.

Your Son,

Gary

They both sat there, just letting it sink in. "Where is the postmark from?" Suzie asked, breaking the silence.

"San Diego, California."

Gary was only sixteen years old. His parents were very worried. They were happy to know, at the time the card was written, Gary was okay, but they wished they had a way to get in touch with him.

After a couple of weeks, Gary decided to move on. He had saved enough money for a bus ticket. Realizing he had enough left to see him through a few days, Gary decided to continue his adventure. He went on to New Mexico. It may not have been the best decision, but he was on his own. Gary was young and wanted to see new places.

In New Mexico his deep sea fishing skills weren't needed, but he did find a lake where they needed some help with smaller boats and rigging. His general fishing knowledge was just what they needed. Gary felt good working in the hot sun. The climate was so different from Oregon and even the California coast. He liked it and decided to stay while.

Periodically he would send notes home. After about six months, he wrote a long letter home. Gary was renting a room at a local boarding house. He was very happy, but did miss home. In closing, he left his address (a local PO Box). Before writing the letter, he decided he would stay and finish out the tourist season. Gary would then return home to be with his family and finish his schooling.

His parents were happy he was coming home. They had been concerned about him and his education. Mathew and Suzie wrote him, hoping to convince Gary to come home sooner. They had not been comfortable with him being on his own. Even now, with all his adventuring under his belt, they would have been a lot happier, if he would have just come home. Where they would have known he was safe. But Gary was safe, and happy too.

The season for lake fishing, in New Mexico, was a lot longer than the season for ocean fishing in Oregon. The days were longer and much hotter. As the season come to a close, he began making plans for his trip back home.

A couple of days before he was supposed to leave, Gary met a girl. She was the most beautiful girl he had ever seen! Her name was Jillianne. She was nineteen and worked as a waitress at the local country club.

The day before he was to leave, Gary asked Jillianne out to lunch. She accepted. He was excited, but very nervous about the date. It was his first official date. Hoping to make a good impression, he practiced how he would act on their date.

Jillianne was nervous as well. She had been on a few dates and normally wasn't uneasy about them. Her nervousness took her by surprise.

Gary met Jillianne were she worked at eleven thirty in the morning. She finished for the day and clocked out. They walked to a nearby café. After an hour of conversation and laughing passed, they decided to take a walk to the lake.

They spent the rest of the day talking. Telling each other all about their growing up and how they came to live here. Gary told her all about his Mother. How she spent most of her time taking care of her family and teaching Gary his studies. He told her about how his Father and Grandfather had been teaching him to be a deep sea fisherman. Then he told her about being shanghaied and his adventures.

Jillianne told Gary how she lost her parents in an airplane crash. How it had been hard to finish high school. But now she had a good job, and was putting herself through night school. She was determined not to be a waitress her whole life.

They spent the afternoon together and on into the evening. It was almost midnight when Gary walked Jillianne home.

The next day, Gary was still reeling from their date. He decided to delay his plans to go back home. Finding himself without a job, he decided to look for work, that morning. It was the off season, which meant there weren't many jobs available. His day of job hunting was disappointing, but he was meeting Jillianne after her last class got out. That lifted his spirits.

From that day on, Gary and Jillianne spent all their free time together. Gary wrote home explaining he had met someone and was planning to stay in New Mexico, through the fall and winter months. His parents were very unhappy that he wouldn't be returning as he had originally planned.

They started planning a trip to see him and meet Jillianne, hoping to convince him to come back with them. Gary was thankful that it would be a few months, at least, before they could come out to visit.

Gary looked for a job every day, for three weeks. His savings were almost depleted, and he thought about going back to Oregon. It was a sad day for him, he wasn't sure how to tell Jillianne, but she brought him some good news. One of the dishwashers at the Country Club was leaving, so there was a job opening. Bright and early the next day Gary went in and got the job, on the spot. It was a great relief to both Gary and Jillianne. Neither one wanted to see Gary go back to Oregon.

Gary was happy to be working. His new job didn't pay as much as the one at the lake, but he was grateful to have a job. He and Jillianne were working in the same restaurant, but their schedules made it difficult to spend time together. Sometimes they would get a shift here and there together, so at least they worked with one another, once in a while. They were glad of that.

As time went on they were becoming very close. They were becoming, not only deeply in love, but best friends. After being together through the fall and the winter months, Gary decided to stay in New Mexico. He went to the lake and was able to get his job back for the spring and summer seasons. It would mean being able to stay, and another letter to Oregon, which was sure to disappoint his parents.

By this time Mathew and Suzie started feeling as though their boy would never return home. The past year had proven to be a very difficult fishing season in Oregon. They would not be able to get to New Mexico for a while, but told Gary to keep in touch and let them know if he needed anything. They encouraged him to finish his education. Hoping he would. It was very hard for them to be so far away, but they were proud of their son's self-reliance.

All spring and summer Gary worked hard, and saved as much money as he could. He didn't want to go back to Oregon in the fall. Gary wanted to stay near Jillianne, and she wanted him to stay, too. At the end of summer, the restaurant owners knew he would be looking for a job, and offered him one. This time the owner of the lake offered him a caretaker's position. It was a hard decision for Gary. It should have been easy. He felt a small loyalty to the restaurant, because they gave him a job when he was desperate for work, but it paid a lot less. Because of his lack of experience in such matters, Gary consulted Jillianne. In the end, he decided it would be best to stay on at the lake. It made a lot more sense, and the restaurant owners were very understanding. They wished him luck.

Gary settled into his new place. As caretaker, he was given small quarters in one of the buildings on the lake property, near the boat dock. His duties were light, most of the time. The boat rental was closed for the fall and winter. The park was open, but the visitors were usually good about keeping it clean. The county was responsible for the maintenance of the main portions of the park. Most of Gary's duties entailed keeping the dock cleaned up and security, especially at night. This allowed him a pretty open schedule during the day.

Jillianne was working hard at the restaurant and started back to school for the fall semester. It wasn't an easy schedule. Gary felt concerned for Jillianne and her tight schedule. He wanted to make her life easier, but there wasn't much he could do. With his new job and better pay, he was able to save more money and take her out, every once in a while.

CHAPTER 3

Time passed. After being in his new position a while, Gary decided he wanted to go a step further with Jillianne. He decided to ask her to marry him. On one particular day, Gary went to the restaurant to see Jillianne. He had lunch and asked her if she would spend the afternoon with him. She said okay, finished up work, and they left.

"Can we go to the mall?" Gary asked.

"Okay?" Jillianne thought it was a strange request. Gary hated the mall.

When they got there, he led her to a jewelry store. "I want to show you something." Gary said. His voice was shaking. He was so nervous. "I want you to pick out a ring."

Jillianne was stunned. "What?!"

"I want you to marry me. Will you...please?"

She didn't know what to say. They were in the middle of the mall, and Gary was on one knee.

It was something she wanted to do, but it was so unexpected. "Yes, I'll marry you. Just get up, you're embarrassing me." She said, with a smile that told him it was okay, but he was very silly.

Gary got up and they went into the store. There were so many rings to choose from. It was so overwhelming. A salesman came up to them, and started showing them some very expensive rings.

"You can have anything you want. My credit is good here. I checked into it yesterday." Gary told Jillianne.

Even though she was happy with the information, and his willingness to go into a lot of debt for her, Jillianne only wanted a simple ring. It was what she had always wanted.

The salesman asked them for a price range. Gary told him two thousand dollars to start, but then Jillianne asked him to start at a hundred dollars. She had to insist, since the salesman only wanted to listen to Gary.

She looked for a long time. Finally, the salesman brought out a selection of very simple elegant rings, and she found the one. It was silver with a heart shaped diamond in the center surrounded with small diamond chips. It was beautiful. Gary was happy because Jillianne was happy. The salesman was disappointed because it was only three hundred and fifty dollars.

They set a date for the next summer. It was far enough away they could save money and plan the wedding. Most important to them both, it gave them time to arrange to fly Gary's family to New Mexico for the wedding.

The next day, Gary called his parents to tell them the good news. He was a bit nervous. Gary was not sure how they would react. He was so young and hadn't been home in so many years. The last time they saw him, he was just sixteen years old. So much had happened to him. Up until the last three years, they had always been a part of Gary's life.

When he got a hold of his family and told them his news, they were shocked. Gary was always shy and timid. This was a different side of him. When he was a child, his parents had been concerned about him socially. Now, they were concerned he was jumping into something, just because he felt safe. What could he really understand about love and commitment to another person? It was a big step, and they weren't sure he should be making it.

They had been hoping he would return home after he was done adventuring. Their plans for Gary had not included him leaving home before his eighteenth birthday, and not finishing high school. Now it seemed, he would not finish high school, get married and settle far from home. Mathew and Suzie were sad about the whole situation, but, as with most parents, their biggest wish was to see him happy. They also figured, he made it this far on his own, so it wasn't their place to intervene.

Gary and Jillianne's life continued in New Mexico. Jillianne worked hard as a waitress and her boss saw it. One day he offered her a promotion, a shift manager. It was more responsibility and an extra hour each day, but the raise in pay that came with it, was worth all the extra effort. She decided to accept the job. Gary was concerned about the extra time she would have to commit to it, with her already hectic schedule. He was hoping things would not get so busy for Jillianne until after she was done with college classes, but this way she was able to save money for their future. That made it worth it.

Gary continued working hard at the lake. He and Jillianne saw each other as often as they could. When he wasn't working or seeing Jillianne, he was studying for his high school diploma, but kept it a secret. He was worried he would be unable to pass it, although he shouldn't have been concerned. Six months after Gary proposed, he went to the local college, took and passed his test for high school diploma. He was so excited he went straight to the country club. Jillianne was working and wouldn't be off for hours, and Gary had to get to work himself. He decided to see if he could pull her aside for a minute. It was very unusual of him, so her boss let her take a short break. When he told her what he had done she was so excited that she told her boss and all the other employees that were there. They all knew Gary, even the new employees. He was around quite a bit, seeing Jillianne still worked there.

The day arrived for Mathew, Suzie and Bill to jump on the plane that would take them to see Gary and meet Jillianne. They were getting married a week after Gary's family was scheduled to arrive. The plan was for his family to spend some time catching up with Gary and getting to know Jillianne, before the ceremony.

As soon as Suzie saw her, she could see how beautiful Jillianne was. Her smile and delicate way about her, told Suzie she must be as sweet as Gary described her. Suzie hoped her first impression of Jillianne was right. All she really wanted was for Gary to be happy and successful in whatever endeavor he chose. She hoped that was what Jillianne wanted for him too.

"Hi Mom! Hi Dad!" Gary shouted across the crowded airport. Soon as they reached each other, he continued. "Where's Grandfather?"

"He headed to baggage. He wanted to give us a minute. This must be the lady we keep hearing about." Mathew said, walking up to Jillianne.

"Dad, Mom, this is Jillianne. Jillianne, this is my Dad, Mathew and my Mom, Suzie."

Jillianne smiled shyly and said, "Hello. I'm pleased to meet you."

After the introductions and friendly hugs, the group proceeded to the baggage claim area to find Bill. Gary couldn't wait to see him and introduce him to Jillianne.

Arriving at the baggage claim area, they found Bill, patiently waiting. Gary ran up and gave him a big hug. He felt like a little boy, in that moment. "Hi, Grandfather. I've missed you!"

Bill just smiled and gave Gary one more hug. His gaze then moved on toward a shy unfamiliar lass. "Who might this be?"

"Excuse me." Gary had almost forgot about everyone else. He was so happy to see his Grandfather. Turning toward her, "This is Jillianne." He said, introducing them.

"My, what a pretty face? You must be the sweetheart, Gary has been telling us about. You look just as kind and lovely as he said." Bill could be very charming, when he wanted to be, but was always sincere.

Jillianne smiled and hugged him.

Gary was happy to see his family accepting Jillianne. He had no doubts, that as they got to know each other, they would love her just as much as a daughter/granddaughter.

After collecting their bags, everyone walked outside to a shuttle pick up area. Gary had scheduled it for them. The shuttle took them to a motel walking distance from the lake. The motel was small, a bit run down, but clean and brightly lit. Soon as everyone was settled in, and after a rest, Gary and Jillianne took everyone out to dinner. It was a wonderful evening.

The next day, Gary had to work. The new season had started, so the owner was back and working with Gary. This enabled him to go back to working shifts, and made it possible to take certain days off. This particular day he was working the day shift, so he would have the afternoon off. Jillianne had the morning free and volunteered to show Mathew, Suzie and Bill around town. Then she would drop them off at the lake and head to work. Gary had reserved a boat for his families' use while he finished work.

When they arrived, Gary was waiting. He had gotten permission to take an extra-long lunch, so that he could spend a little time with everyone. Jillianne had stopped at the local deli on the way to the lake. She bought sandwiches, salad and drinks for all of them to share. After eating, Jillianne left for work. Then Gary took his family and showed them around.

Before returning to work, he made sure everyone was comfortable on the boat. Dad, Mom and Bill trolled the lake, from one end to the other. All three loved the setting. It was very different from the waters of the Pacific Ocean.

CHAPTER 4

Bill and Mathew decided to try their hand at lake fishing. They had done a little back home, but even the lakes and rivers were different. They had good luck and caught their limits. All the while, Suzie was reading a book and enjoying the scenery. It was a very nice afternoon.

She enjoyed the quietness and beauty of the lake, and was impressed with Gary's new skills. Suzie saw how he incorporated his old fishing skills into his new job. Her pride in him was abundant. The way he handled himself and his responsibilities, proved to her, regardless of his age, he was no longer a boy, but a full grown man.

Mathew saw how well he worked with the public and was no longer worried about him socializing with the rest of the world. He saw some of the challenges and great responsibilities that were entrusted to his son. Gary met them head on and passed with flying colors. Mathew too, was very proud of his son.

Bill watched for a long time. He saw Gary

work hard, use his skills and interact with people. Although Gary's parents were quick to tell him how proud they were, Bill said nothing about his feelings toward how Gary was doing. He didn't feel it was time.

When his work was done, Gary and his family went to dinner at the club were Jillianne was working. They had a wonderful meal. When Jillianne's shift ended, she was able to join them. Jillianne's boss (Gary's old boss, too) came to their table just as they were finishing desert. And to their surprise, he told them dinner was on the house. It was the restaurant's wedding present to the two of them.

The next few days were busy. Jillianne and Gary were finalizing their wedding plans. Gary was able to get three days off, with the days he normally had off, it gave him a week. He worked up to two days before the wedding. The three days following would give them a mini honey moon. Jillianne was able to get more time off. Two weeks! She spent time with Suzie getting things ready. Mathew and Bill spent a lot of time at the lake helping Gary with his work. It enabled him to get off work earlier in the day. Mathew and Bill got to spend time with Gary and be near the water. Besides, they were happy to stay out of the wedding planning, for the most part.

Suzie and Jillianne really enjoyed their time together. Jillianne couldn't help thinking of Suzie as her Mother, rather than a soon to be, Mother-in-law. This suited Suzie just fine, because she felt the same. An important bond that was forming.

Jillianne longed for a family. She was happy to see she was coming into one that seemed so loving and caring. One day, as they sat outside an ice cream shop, resting and eating ice cream. Jillianne told Suzie how she lost her parents in an airplane crash. "They loved to go flying, and had their own plane. Dad and Mom went out one day. Out of nowhere a storm came up, an electrical one. The instruments went berserk. My Dad lost control of the plane. It plunged into the sand in the middle of the desert. They died on impact."

When Jillianne finished her story she was visibly shaken. Suzie took her hand. "I don't want to replace your Mother. I'm sure I couldn't, if I wanted to, but I would like to be a second Mother to you. I would like to be there for you, when you want a mother's advice or confidence. I have enjoyed our short time together, and grown very fond of you. I will be proud to call you, Daughter."

A smile came to Jillianne's face and tears weld up in her eyes. She didn't speak, for fear of being unable to control her emotions, but walked over to hug her. The two women stood in an embrace. Then, realizing they were outside an ice cream shop, stopped, looked at each other and giggled. How silly they felt. It was a nice tension breaker.

The next morning, after breakfast and when the fellas were gone, Jillianne asked Suzie if she wanted to see her wedding dress.

"Oh, yes. I would love to." Suzie said, with a smile.

The two ladies walked to Jillianne's bedroom. Jillianne opened the box on the bed. As she did, Jillianne smiled with a bit of sadness in her eyes. "It was my Mother's. I had it cleaned and tailored to fit me."

As she held it up, Suzie looked on in awe. It was ivory. Princess cut, with a high neck. Lace covered every inch and the sleeves were long, all the way to the base of her fingers. At the waist, pearl beads were sewn along the seam to show off the waist line. The train was of the same lace, trimmed in pearl beads and satin roses dotted a line from her waist to the end of the train. When it was out the roses were spaced apart, but when the train was pinned up the roses were in a close line together.

Jillianne tried it on so Suzie could see it. She was beautiful!

"Do you have a veil?" Suzie asked.

"No, I don't. I was just going to put my hair up. I have two silver combs that were my mother's." Jillianne's eyes started to tear up as she thought of her Mother.

"How pretty that will be. Would it be alright if I bought you a veil to go with your combs?" Suzie hoped she could get her something to make her day that much more special.

Jillianne smiled. "That would make everything perfect! Thank you."

Suzie helped her put the dress back in the box. Then they took it with them to find a veil to match. It took most of the day to shop. After a long while, and Jillianne trying dozens, they found a veil. It was a perfect match. During their shopping, Jillianne took Suzie to her favorite second hand clothing store. It had the most beautiful, gently used clothing. Suzie found a dress for the wedding. She had brought a plain green dress that she wore to church sometimes. It was very practical and a bit on the warm side for New Mexico. But this dress, was beautiful. It was a brilliant blue cotton with deep blue accents. A mature style, fitted and very flattering.

"Won't Mathew be surprised when you show him?" Jillianne said, with a wink.

They both smiled and giggled a little.

"Can I treat you to lunch?" Suzie asked.

"You've done so much already."

"I would really like to. It would mean so much to me."

"Okay, I would love to." Jillianne said, enthusiastically.

After lunch, they stopped to reserve three tuxes. They chose blue for the ties and comber buns for Mathew and Bill, to match Suzie's dress. Then they chose black for Gary's tux. As they finished, they realized it was getting close to the time the fellas were to arrive home, but Suzie wanted to make one more stop. "Where can we find a good flower shop?"

Jillianne smiled. "We are okay without flowers. I was going to pick some the morning of the wedding."

"It's okay. I planned on buying them." Suzie smiled, chuckled to herself and said. "By the way, I got off easy, I had planned to buy you a dress." She was very happy Jillianne had her mother's wedding dress.

Jillianne showed Suzie to a flower shop in an out of the way spot. It had been recommended to her by her boss. They ordered a bridal bouquet for Jillianne, a smaller bouquet for the bride's maid and a corsage for Suzie to match. Then Suzie purchased three boutonnieres for the fellas.

The bouquets were made of blue and purple wild flowers with white roses for accents. Suzie's corsage was a single rose with a few wild flowers. The boutonnieres were single white roses. Jillianne was so excited to have professionally done flowers at her wedding. All the way home she was smiling. Jillianne couldn't wait to tell Gary about her day.

It was so late, that they bought pizza on the way home. Late as it was the fellas got to Jillianne's about the same time as they did.

Jillianne was so excited she was bursting with the news of the day. Gary stepped out of the vehicle. She ran up, hugging him, she started telling him all about her day with his mother! It was very hard for Jillianne to contain all her excitement, but she did, not wanting to overwhelm Gary. Everyone was very pleased to see Jillianne and Suzie so happy.

While they sat eating and talking, Gary spoke up. "I have something to tell everyone."

He looked nervous. Jillianne got scared, thinking he might be having second thoughts. That same thought was running through everyone else's minds too.

"I just wanted you all to know, I received my high school diploma. I've had it for a while, but I waited to say anything, until we were all together."

Everyone was very happy. Jillianne didn't mind that Gary had waited to tell everyone together and neither did anyone else.

Soon it was the day of the wedding, Jillianne and Susie went by the florist on the way to the Lake. The men went to pick up their tuxes, and would all meet at the marina.

Gary got permission to have their ceremony at one of the picnic spots surrounding the lake. Suzie, and some of Jillianne's friends came early to decorate.

It was a small wedding only about 10 or 12 people (including the wedding party). The ceremony went off without a hitch. It was beautiful! Everyone was so happy. After the ceremony, the wedding moved to a pontoon boat with music and hors d'oeuvres and of course they had a wedding cake. They stayed on the water for a couple of hours. Gary had a radio/disc player on the boat so they could dance. They played a special song for Gary and Jillianne to dance to. Then Mathew and Bill took turns dancing with Jillianne and Gary danced with Suzie. Everyone had a good time, but they were exhausted at the end of the evening.

After the wedding, Jillianne's friends cleaned up. It was their wedding present. It was perfect. It allowed Gary and Jillianne to go to Jillianne's house as soon as the reception was over. It also gave Mathew, Suzie and Grandfather a chance to go back to the hotel and get a restful night's sleep. They were going back to Oregon in the morning.

Gary and Jillianne had a wonderful evening. Gary, even carried her over the threshold. They were so happy to be able to stay together all night. "Guess what," Jillianne said, grinning. "It's three in the morning. Don't you think you had better leave? I want to stay respectable, you know?"

"We're married now. You can't get rid of me that easily, anymore." Gary said, tickling his new bride. They both giggled, feeling a bit silly.

The next morning, Gary and Jillianne took Mathew, Suzie and Bill out to breakfast, before heading to the airport. After they said tearful good-byes, Gary and Jillianne went back home to finish packing. Then they were off on a three-day honeymoon.

They drove up to a small cabin in a remote part of the mountains. On the way up, Gary had made reservations at a quiet romantic restaurant. It was beautiful.

When they reached the cabin, Jillianne brought out champagne and strawberries. They had a very romantic evening. The next day, they went hiking. They found a remote part of the river and went skinny dipping. It was a first for both of them. Gary and Jillianne spent all their time goofing off and just hanging out. Their honeymoon was the nice quiet vacation they both needed. It gave them time to connect, and just be a couple. They were sad to see it end, but of course, work was calling.

CHAPTER 5

They were married about a year when Gary and Jillianne decided it was time for a much needed vacation. Everything was going well in their lives. It was busy with work and Jillianne's schooling. When Jillianne finished college and started on her career, they planned for Gary to start college. It was a good plan. So before the next term started, Gary planned a trip for them to visit his family in Depoe Bay, Oregon.

On the day of the trip Gary was frantic. "Jillianne, I can't find my mom's present!"

Jillianne looked calmly at him. "I already packed it in my suitcase." Gary's face softened as Jillianne continued. "I wanted to make sure it wasn't forgotten."

Gary had searched and searched for a present for his mother. She was very special to him. All those years of raising him and caring for him. Gary always felt he owed her something, but not because she made him feel that way. Suzie was just that kind of mom. She felt it was her privilege to raise and care for her child. This made, making sure he got his perfect gift to her, that much more important. It was a vase with a bright red cardinal. It was her favorite of all the birds she saw while visiting last year.

"It's getting late. Are you about ready?" Gary sounded stressed, again.

"All the bags are packed and by the door. I am just tidying up the kitchen."

"Good, the taxi should be here in a few minutes."

"I'll be ready." Jillianne said, finishing the dishes. After the dishes, she started sweeping the floor. As she was finishing, she heard the taxi pull up. Soon after, the bell started ringing. Then she heard Gary get up and answer the door. Jillianne put the broom and dust pan away, went into the living room, and grabbed her things. "I'm ready, sweetie."

Gary came in from putting their bags into the taxi. He grabbed his coat and walked out the door, hand in hand with Jillianne. The airport was its usual mass of people and confusion. They made it through security with time to spare. It was an uneventful flight, and they arrived at the Portland airport right on time. Then rented a car and were off to Depoe Bay.

Jillianne was very excited to see all the places Gary had told her so much about. As they drove along she was amazed at how green and lush everything was. Even around the airport things were green. Gary took her on a side trip down Marine Drive, just long enough to see the Columbia River Gorge. They looked across the river and saw Washington State. Then it was time to hop on the freeway that would take them to their destination.

It was about a two and half hour ride to get there. Since the flight and car ride took so long, they decided to stop for a bite. About halfway there, they stopped at a Dairy Queen restaurant that seemed to be in the middle of nowhere. Gary had told Jillianne about how they would stop at the restaurant, when he was a little boy, on the way to or from Portland. It was a nice break about halfway.

After their meal, and a short rest, Gary and Jillianne were on their way. They grew more excited as each mile passed by. Although, Gary was a little anxious. He wasn't sure how people would perceive him, after his long absence. His anxiety was unwarranted. The only people that really mattered, loved him for who he was, and knew what kind of a person he was.

Jillianne felt very fortunate and content. She missed Gary's family. It pleased her, to be able to remind herself, it was her family to. They had accepted her fully into their group.

"Here we are in Lincoln city." Gary said, interrupting Jillianne's thoughts. "Just about 12 or 13 miles and we will be in Depoe Bay."

"Oh, I can hardly wait."

As they traveled down highway 101 thru Lincoln City, Jillianne saw her first glimpse of the ocean. She was overcome with amazement. Gary could see the excitement in her eyes. He looked for the next turn off that would give them access to the ocean. Next to the D sands motel there was a turnoff with stairs that gave access to the beach. As Gary drove the car toward the turnoff, Jillianne looked somewhat confused.

"I thought you might enjoy taking a break, and feel the sand between your toes." Gary said with a smile.

"I've never seen the ocean before, or felt sand between my toes. Well, not beach sand."

Jillianne was referring to the desert sands of New Mexico.

Gary and Jillianne spent almost an hour walking up and down the beach. Dodging in and out of waves. The weather was beautiful. It was a bright sunny day, not over cast at all. As luck might have it, the tide pools were visible. They had come just at the right time, low tide. It was such a wonderful experience for Jillianne. Gary showed her how the animals hid in the crevices of the little pools, where the water would become trapped, as the waves rushed in. He explained to her how the food that came in on the waves would become trapped in the pools. The mollusks and other sea creatures would feed on it. Jillianne was even lucky enough to see some starfish. Gary explained how there was a law in Oregon that stated nothing was to be removed from the tide pools. People used to come and collect little animals. It was harmful to them. Many of them died, just from being pulled off the rocks they were attached to, even though most people put them right back. The creatures' numbers were dwindling before the law. Now they were thriving.

They decided it was time to continue on their journey to Gary's childhood home. As they got in the car, Jillianne looked way out over the ocean. "Gary, what is that?"

Gary followed her gaze and was very excited. "That's a whale! How lucky!"

Jillianne talked the rest of the way to Gary's parents' house. She was overwhelmed with the beach, the waves, the tide pools and seeing a whale for the first time. It was so much more than she had ever expected.

Before Jillianne realized it, they were turning off the highway onto a small road near the harbor. Soon, they were at their destination. It was just as Gary had described it. The house was a classic old Main style home complete with cedar siding. Jillianne thought, "How beautiful," as she stepped out of the car.

A few minutes later she and Gary were ringing the doorbell. Suzie answered. Everyone exchanged hellos and hugs. Suzie brought Gary and Jillianne into the living room where Bill and Mathew were sitting going over maps. They all smiled, as they came together in the center of the room. More hellos and hugs were exchanged. It was a very warm and friendly gathering.

Later, after Gary and Jillianne all were

settled in, everyone gathered back in the living room to relax and reconnect with each other.

"So how was your trip?" Mathew asked.

"Oh, it was wonderful!" Jillianne was still excited. She had never been anywhere but New Mexico. "I love how green, everything is here. Gary stopped so that we could wander the beach together. We were only there for a short time, and I saw so many things! I saw the tide pools, driftwood, shells and some beautiful rocks. Oh, of course, the ocean." Jillianne giggled. "Just as we were about to leave, I got a glimpse of a whale." Her voice trailed off. She realized she had been babbling. Feeling a little silly and self-conscious, she got very quiet. Everyone understood. This was her first great adventure. They were happy to see her excitement and feel the energy that poured out from her.

Jillianne regained her composure and began to speak again. "I am very happy to see all of you. I miss having you around me." She paused. "Thank you, for letting us come and visit." She was smiling again and happy to be there.

While Gary started talking to his Father and Grandfather, Suzie got up to fix some refreshments for everyone. Jillianne got up and followed her. "Don't worry, dear, about being so excited and talkative. We are happy you are enjoying your trip." Suzie said, once they were in the kitchen.

Jillianne smiled and felt better.

Back in the living room, the fellas were talking and catching up. Gary asked about that year's fishing. "They aren't biting like they were last year, but still a good catch." Mathew said.

"Do you think we could take the boat out tomorrow?" Gary asked.

"Sure, would Jillianne like to come?" Bill inquired.

Gary wasn't sure if he wanted Jillianne to come along. It wasn't that he didn't want to share his fishing time with her. He just missed fishing with his Father and Grandfather, just the way they did when he was a boy.

Jillianne came in just as they were discussing who was to come along and saw the undecided look on Gary's face. "Thank you for thinking of me, Bill, but I was hoping to spend some 'girl time' with Mom."

"Well then," Mathew said, "it's all set. The guys on the boat and the girls in town."

Everyone was happy.

The next day, five a.m. came, and everyone was up. The girls were getting coffee and breakfast on the table. While, the guys were gathering equipment and lunches, the girls had made.

"Come, sit at the table. Your food is getting cold." Susie said, sounding like her old self.

"Oh, how I've missed this." Gary thought to himself. "How could it get any better than this?" Gary was very happy, but the realization of this situation being only temporary, made him sad. When vacation was over, he and Jillianne would have to return to New Mexico. He knew he missed his boyhood home, but never realized how much, until that very moment.

Gary went fishing with his Father and Grandfather. It felt just like old times. Being, he was still, 'low man on the totem pole', Gary still had to earn position. It was just as it should be.

Jillianne and Suzie cleaned up after breakfast. Then went out to run errands. They weren't exciting, just things like grocery shopping or picking up a few things for the house. They enjoyed spending the time together.

Suzie took her out to lunch at Gracie's. "So this is the famous Gracie's Sea Hag, Gary's told me so much about." Jillianne was happy to be there. It was chock full of local history and the food, fantastic! "I could spend all day looking at the old fishing pictures on the walls and reading the articles that accompany many of them. Thank you, Mom, for taking me here."

When Jillianne and Gary saw each other, at the end of the day, they had some interesting stories. They were anxious to share with each other, but they waited until after dinner.

It was a warm evening. Perfect, for a walk along the beach. They walked for a long time, just holding hands, listening to the surf and feeling close to one another. After a while, Jillianne began telling Gary about what a wonderful day she had with his Mom. About shopping and Gracie's Sea Hag. She let Gary know how much she missed his family, and said it might be good to think about coming back to stay.

Then it was Gary's turn to tell Jillianne how much he enjoyed his day. He hadn't realized he missed his parents and Grandfather and the family fishing business, so much.

At the end of their conversation, they had decided as soon as they got back home, they would come up with a plan to move to Oregon in the next 3 to 5 years. It had been a good day that ended with a special night.

The next day at breakfast, Gary casually mentioned their intended plans. Everyone was ecstatic. During the rest of their visit, it was the most talked about subject. The week went by faster than anyone would have liked. Knowing Gary and Jillianne would be back to stay, in a few short years, made their leaving less painful.

The day before their flight, Gary and Jillianne headed to Portland. After long sad goodbyes and I'll miss you tears, they headed down the highway. Gary decided to surprise her with one more of Oregon's natural wonders. He took her to see Multnomah Falls, before heading to their hotel, close to the airport. Jillianne had never seen a waterfall so high. They took the trail to a bridge half way up to the top. It was so beautiful, it nearly took her breath away. Oregon, Jillianne concluded, was the most beautiful place she had ever been. The next day they got on the airplane, sad to be leaving, but excited for their future.

The next three years were good ones. Full of spending time together, planning for their future and saving for their new life in Oregon. Gary and Jillianne planned to start a family as soon as they were settled in their new home, but their plans got changed. About six months before their planned move, Jillianne came to Gary. "Guess what?!"

"What?" Gary asked.

"I'm pregnant!" She was very excited, but concerned about how Gary would feel. Because they were still in New Mexico, this would change their plans, quite a bit.

Gary was very happy and a little nervous. He knew it wasn't exactly the way they planned it. They would have to post-pone their moving plans, but what better reason could they have?!

Soon as the shock wore off a little, they called home to tell Gary's family. By the end of the conversation, Suzie and Mathew were talking about coming down, soon as the baby was born. Mathew would have about a week before returning home to help Bill with the fishing business. Suzie would stay behind a while to help with the house and the baby.

After the talk with Gary's parents, they felt more at ease about being able to care for the baby while preparing to move. They pushed their moving date farther out. It would be hard to look for work and find a place to live with a brand new baby, so they decided to move when the baby was about six months to a year old.

At first everything went right on schedule. Jillianne planned to work throughout the pregnancy. When time got close, she would quit, in order to stay home to take care of the baby and to begin preparations for moving. About six months in to the pregnancy, things started to get difficult. Jillianne was having issues. It started with gestational diabetes. The doctors told her to take it easy and work shorter hours. Gary and Jillianne decided not to take any chances. She quit her job, earlier than expected, so she could take care of herself and the unborn baby.

A week later she started finding little bits of blood when she used the restroom. The doctor said it was normal to spot sometimes. A few days later, the spotting, became pretty consistent. Jillianne's doctor put her on bed rest. With instructions to go straight to the hospital, if it got any worse. Two days later it did, and Gary took her to the emergency department.

It was the middle of the night. Jillianne was scared. Gary was too, but tried not to show it. He wanted her to stay calm. They took her in as soon as she entered the hospital. Gary followed close behind, careful to stay out of the way. They whisked her into an operating room. Gary was stopped at the door. "You'll have to wait outside. I'm sorry." The nurse said, looking at him thoughtfully.

Gary went to a private waiting room. It was smaller than a normal waiting room. The hospital had a few set up so the family could wait and worry in peace. Soon as he was alone, Gary called his folks.

Mathew woke up to the phone ringing. "Hello." He said groggily.

"Hey, dad…" Gary sounded strained and very scared.

Mathew immediately lost his grogginess. "What's wrong? What's going on, son?!"

Gary was in a haze, pacing back and forth, as he explained Jillianne's condition. "I don't know anymore…Just a minute, the nurse is here…I'll have to call you back." Without saying good-bye, or waiting for a response from his dad, Gary hung up the phone.

"I'm sorry," she began, "We lost the baby." She waited while the news sunk in. Just as she was about to speak again...

Gary interrupted her, "How's Jillianne?!"

She began again. "Your wife is hemorrhaging. The doctors are having a hard time getting the bleeding stopped. I'll be back as soon as her condition changes." The nurse paused and put a hand on Gary's shoulder. "Do you need anything? Can I call someone for you?" The nurse was very kind and sympathetic.

Gary didn't answer. He just looked at her, but the nurse understood. She had seen the same look, in the eyes of other worried family members, before. Without saying anymore, she left. Gary was a bit relieved. It was hard enough to cope, without an audience.

The next half hour felt like several hours. He paced. Sat in a chair. Fidgeted. Paced some more. Just as he sat down for the tenth time, the nurse came back in, but this time the doctor came too. They didn't have to say a word, but Gary waited to hear the doctor say it. He was hoping and praying he had misread their expressions. The doctor's words came to Gary as in a dream. "She's gone. I'm sorry. We did everything we could." The doctor reached out to touch Gary's shoulder, but stopped. He could see by his body language that it wouldn't help and wasn't welcomed.

"Thank you. I would like to see them." Gary said emphatically, expecting them to say no.

"You'll have to wait here. The nurse will come and get you when it is time." The doctor hated this part of his job, but he preferred talking to someone like Gary. He was straight to the point and wanted the information the same way. It somehow made his job slightly easier.

After a while the nurse came back, and took him to see his wife and child. Gary needed the conformation that they were truly gone. He needed to say good-bye. Looking at them, he picked up their little girl. He held their child for the first and last time. Gary cradled her in his arms, then hugged and kissed her good-bye. The nurse took the baby from his arms as carefully as if she were alive and breathing. Gary held Jillianne for a long time. Then stroked her forehead, just as he had done so many times before, but for the last time, kissed her and whispered, "Good-bye, my sweet angel."

Looking up at the caring nurse, he handed her a note that he had written while waiting to come to this room. It read: Please call Mathew Jones. He will make the arrangements. The rest of the note had contact information. Then he turned, and walked out. Out of the room. Out of the hospital, and out of life.

CHAPTER 6

Gary went missing for almost two weeks. He wondered the desert, with only a pack. Not caring about anything. Giving up was all he wanted to do, but his spirit wouldn't let him.

Everyone was very worried about him. When Mathew received the call from the hospital, he knew Gary had left town. Suzie wanted to rush to New Mexico to be with Gary. Mathew and Bill convinced her to wait. They knew she would be wasting her time trying to find him. If she did find him, he needed the space right now, not his mother.

When Gary returned to life, everything he did or saw reminded him of Jillianne, and the life they would have had with their child. It was all he could do, just to go back to their house. He couldn't eat. He couldn't sleep. The job he abandoned was still there, if he wanted it, but he didn't want it. Gary didn't know what he wanted. His spirit wouldn't let him give up completely, so he decided it was time for a change. It was time to go home, to Oregon, and clear his head.

He contacted his parents. Suzie was relieved and very happy to know he was okay. His Father was happy he called, and was ready to come home. Bill invited Gary to live with him, as long as he wanted. They all loved him very much and were there to support him. Mathew and Bill also knew, Gary would have to stand on his own, to recover from losing his family. He sold most everything, even the car, and jumped on a plane to Oregon.

Throwing himself into work with his Father and Grandfather, he repaired nets, sorted and reorganized everything on the boat. When that was done, Gary started all the little repairs that Mathew and Bill never had time to get to. The boat had never been so 'ship shape'. It was a wonderful distraction. On one of his many sleepless nights, Gary could be found working on the boat.

Mathew was proud of his son for not giving up on life. He knew the difficulty and strain Gary was under. Every day he struggled to find a reason to get out of bed. If it wasn't for his family and being able to work on the boat, Gary didn't know what he would have done.

The baby's due date arrived. He worked on the boat that day and all the next. He didn't even stop to eat or sleep. This trend continued. Gary fell into a deep depression. After a couple of days, he began eating, but barely. A few weeks went by and things were the same. Suzie decided it was time she came to see him.

It was about nine o'clock in the morning, when she arrived. Gary looked as though he hadn't changed his clothing, in at least a week. He sat at the galley table staring into his coffee cup. It appeared as though he hadn't been to bed in weeks, either.

"It's time you went out to lunch with your Mom." Suzie said, smiling. She was hoping to get him out and into the fresh air.

"I would really rather be alone today. I hope you understand." Gary was very calm and quiet.

His Mom was unsure if it would really be best for him to be alone, but not knowing what to do or wanting to interfere with his wishes, she said good-bye. Touching his shoulder and giving him a motherly kiss, she left, hoping he would work things out.

Gary sat for a long time lost in thoughts from his past, in New Mexico. Before he knew it, it was twelve o'clock. He decided he had moped long enough. His Mother coming by, would have been just what Jillianne would have wanted. Gary could imagining her saying, "Gary, get off your, butt! When life is hard or heart breaking, you can't let it win. Get out of those nasty clothes, shower and shave. Then take your worried Mother and Father out for dinner!"

Gary knew he should get his shit together. He called his Mother to invite his parents to dinner. Then made reservations. When the arrangements were made, Gary jumped into the shower, emerging a less depressed man.

Dinner helped get him out of his funk. He had been contemplating what to do next. Maybe a job in town, he wasn't sure. At dinner Gary discussed it with his parents, and found that Grandfather was having some health issues related to getting older. His balance was off quite a bit, his eyesight was not very good and he was beginning to forget things. Gary had been staying on the boat, and didn't notice Bill's decline. It was a surprise to Gary. Mathew and Suzie had hoped he would stay with the fishing boat, at least, through fishing season, working it full time and give Bill more time to address his issues. It sounded great to Gary. So it was decided, he would continue fishing on the boat and stay nights at his Grandfather's house.

Bill and Gary were sitting in the living room one evening. "Grandson, I know this last year has been quite hard for you. It was really difficult for me, after your Grandmother passed away, but I couldn't give up on life. I had your Father to look after."

"How did you do it?"

"I did just what you've been doing. I kept myself busy."

"Grandfather, when does the pain go away?" He sounded like a small boy asking.

"Well, son, it never really goes away, but it does become less...less noticeable. I mean, it's easier to push the memories away, and concentrate on the now. To look to the future and not the past...so much." Bill's thoughts started drifting back to when he lost his wife. Snapping back into reality, he patted his Grandson's knee. "You'll be fine. It just takes time."

The conversation with Bill helped Gary. He felt less alone, knowing his Grandfather understood and would be there for him.

For the next year, Gary worked hard and saved. He wanted to better himself. To do that, he needed to go to college. While he worked, he took time thinking about what classes he wanted to sign up for. He loved the ocean and all the wondrous creatures in and around it. After careful consideration, he chose to major in Ocean, Earth and Atmospheric Sciences and minor in Marine Resource Management. Soon as fishing season was over, Gary started the process for entering college. He applied for a student loan and took the entrance exams at the local community college. They were a little nerve racking, but he passed with high marks in every subject. Gary was even able to bypass a few of the basic classes.

School was good for him. It enabled him to bury himself in his studies. Gary could feel his confidence and will, to live life, returning. School had helped begin the healing process.

The first year, even though he was able to bypass some classes, Gary still had many prerequisites to take. He enjoyed his science and math classes, but writing and literary classes bored him. The rest of his classes had their interesting and boring days. All in all, he was very happy to be in school.

When his semester was over, and fishing season was beginning, he was back on the boat.

Fishing was their family's way of life, and Gary was good at it. Mathew and Suzie were happy he was following his own interests. Grandfather was especially proud of his achievements. Sometimes Gary felt he would be letting his family down by not continuing their fishing tradition. One day they were discussing things and his family made it abundantly clear, he was not letting them down. It was decided by Gary, with the blessing of his family, during the off season he would continue with his education. During the fishing season he would work on the boat. After graduation, he would look for a job in the field of Oceanography.

Gary had a good life of growing and healing over the next two years. It felt nice being able to help his family. He and Grandfather were happy to be together, living under the same roof. Every day he felt his sadness fade a little. Gary still missed Jillianne, but had learned to concentrate on happy memories. He learned to be grateful for the time they had together. The blue days became fewer and farther between. Happy days out numbering sad ones. His deeply depressed feelings began to only present themselves during holidays and anniversaries. The rest of the year, sadness came and went in short felt waves.

CHAPTER 7

The last year of junior college he was short a credit, but it was an elective. It was nice to be able to choose, just about any class, to fill the credit. Gary was tired from the work load his more difficult classes had given him. In order to relieve stress, he decided on an art class. He was looking forward to the beginning of class, but had no idea what he was in for.

Gary arrived about five minutes early, found a seat and got out his sketch pad. He was busily looking through his things, hoping he hadn't forgotten anything, when in walked a familiar face. It was Alice, and to his surprise, she was the teacher! Gary was excited to see his old friend.

Alice was away when Gary came home. She had been awarded a scholarship to a four year program at a liberal arts college. Alice had become an art major with a minor in English literature. After she returned to the area, they both ran in different circles. They never bumped into each other until that day in class. It just happened that Alice needed some extra money to finance a project she was working on. Teaching at the local college gave her an opportunity to earn the money and allowed her to use one of the art studios, after class.

When Alice saw Gary, she smiled. The bell rang, and class started. "Good afternoon, I am Alice Jenkins. Welcome to my class." She had such a sweet voice. "Just to be sure you are in the right class, this is basic art 101. If you are in the wrong class please take this time to go and find your correct class."

One person stood up, apologized, and left looking very frustrated.

"Now let's go around the room and introduce ourselves."

Everyone took turns saying hello and their name. When it came time for Gary to introduce himself, he said hello and his name. As much as he wanted to chat with Alice, that would have to come after class.

Gary enjoyed this first class. She was a good teacher, keeping everyone involved. Alice taught with excitement, and was genuinely interested in the class' work and their opinions.

When the bell rang to end class Gary waited

for everyone to file out. Then approached Alice. "Hi."

Alice smiled.

"I haven't seen you in years. How have you been?"

"Good." Alice said. "How have you been?" As she and Gary were talking, Alice was walking around the room setting up for her next class.

"I've been well." Gary said, as he started helping Alice, following her lead.

"I would really like to talk and catch up, but I have another class coming in soon." Alice seemed really disappointed.

"When are you done with classes?"

"About six o'clock."

"Can I meet you somewhere for dinner? My treat." Gary said smiling.

"Sounds great, but would you mind meeting me back here? I usually take the bus home."

"Of course, that would be just fine. What time?"

"Six fifteen. That will give me time to clean up after class."

"See you then." Gary said smiling as he left the classroom.

He had some time to kill, so Gary went home, changed his shirt and freshened up. Taking time to tidy up his car, he barely made it back by six fifteen.

She was happy to see he was back, and almost on time. Alice noticed he had cleaned up a bit. "What a change from the scruffy kid I used to know." She said to herself.

"Are you ready? Is there something I can help you with?" Gary asked as he watched Alice putting things away.

"Thank you, but I'll just be a minute. Would you take this, please?" She asked, handing him a giant sketch pad. Alice finished gathering her things, and they were out the door.

"Where would you like to eat?" Gary asked.

"Do you remember that quiet little Mom and Pop restaurant down by the harbor?"

"Yes, that sounds good." Gary remembered

the quaint little spot. He and Alice used to fish off the dock that surrounded the restaurant. It held many happy memories for them.

When they got there they found a nice corner booth. Gary and Alice ordered, ate and talked. They talked for hours. One of the owners came over to their table. "I'm sorry to interrupt. I noticed how much you are enjoying each other's company, but we closed half an hour ago."

"Oh, we're sorry." Gary said, looking at his watch. "Wow, it's after ten o'clock!"

They had been enjoying their time together so much, time had just flown by. Gary quickly paid the check, and they left. On the way to Alice's house, they made plans to go out the next week, after her last art class of the day. This continued every week. By mid-semester, Gary and Alice were seeing each other on class nights and three or four other times throughout the weekdays and on most weekends.

The end of the semester came and Gary graduated. He was supposed to move away to Oregon State University in the fall. Recently, he had begun to rethink his plans. Grandfather was getting older and Gary felt it would be better if he stayed with him at night. Luckily, the University was only about an hour and a half away. It would allow him to come home in the evening and on the weekends. His Father and Mother were still close by and would be able to check in with him during the weekdays. It would also give him a chance to see more of Alice. Of course, that had nothing to do with his decision.

Alice took the summer semester off, from teaching, to work on her art. Finding time to see each other was easier, because her schedule became more flexible and Gary was out of school until fall. His only obligation was to work on the boat. They were able to meet for dinner a couple times a week, and on the weekends they spent a lot of time together.

Alice told him how she had always loved to draw and work with clay, but had never looked at it more than just a hobby. When it came time to decide on a college and a major, Alice wasn't sure what she wanted. She had high marks in most of her studies. Art College wasn't even a consideration, but one day her Mom came to her, she had noticed how much Alice enjoyed creating things. She suggested Alice look into a subject area that had creativity and away for her to express herself. With the blessings of her parents she was free to pursue a degree in visual art. The more she researched art degrees, she found there was so much more to learn than she thought. Originally, she was going to take English literature as her major, with a minor in art, but that soon changed. It made more sense to her, and her happiness, to flip her major and minor around.

She really enjoyed learning something she was passionate about. Whenever she spoke about any aspect of the art world, her eyes sparkled with excitement! Gary loved just listening to her. He found himself fully absorbed in her every word. Art had always been just something to pass the time for him, but not for Alice, she made it come alive. By the end of summer, he found his interest in art, and in Alice, had become more than a passing fancy.

As they grew closer, Gary was able to share some pieces of his past. He shared, in detail his adventures while being shanghaied, how he traveled around and his job at the lake in New Mexico, but stopped short when he got to the part where he met Jillianne. He never opened up to anyone about it. It was just too painful to go through descriptions and explanations. Even in conversations with his family, about Jillianne, he was very closed off.

CHAPTER 8

Fall semester brought teaching for Alice. She was moving out of state to be a student teacher for the fall, winter and spring semesters at her previous art school. It would complete her training, and she would receive her degree in Liberal Arts. Fall semester would find Gary working toward his degree also, but when he finished, he would still have three years to go.

This was the first fishing season he would miss, since he came back from New Mexico. He had moved to the freshman dormitory the day before classes began. That way he was able to see Alice as much as he could before they both had to leave Depoe Bay. The classes he needed to complete his degree program were limited. The only series they offered, started in the fall. He felt sad not helping on the boat, but he knew this is where he belonged. At least he thought so, until he got a call from his Mother.

The weather started out more turbulent than usual this season. Gary had been talking to his Father during the preceding weeks. Mathew had complained that the sea was choppy and more treacherous than he could ever remember. He wondered if he should be taking Bill out on the boat this season, or maybe hire a younger man. It would have been the first time ever to hire anyone that wasn't family. In the end, Bill wouldn't hear of it, and they decided to fish this season together.

Gary had just walked into his room, coming from his morning classes, when the phone started ringing. "I've been trying to reach you for hours!" It was his Mother. She sounded very scared, as panic came through, loud and clear over the phone line.

"What is it?" Gary was very nervous. He was afraid of what his Mother would say next.

"Your Father and Grandfather went out on calm seas this morning. All of a sudden a storm blew in from nowhere...They're missing." The words caught in her throat.

Gary was beside himself with fear. "I'll be there as soon as I can." He said trying to sound calm and reassuring. "It'll be okay. It's early yet. They'll find them."

"I know your right, son."

"I'll see you soon. I love you."

"I love you too." Suzie managed to get the words out and hang up the phone before the tears started streaming down her face, again.

As he hung up with Suzie, Gary's mind was racing. Thankfully, it was Friday. He would have a couple of days before he had to go back to class. Grabbing a couple of things, he headed out to his car. Gary raced to his parents' home. It took him less than the normal hour and a half. During the drive, all he could think about was how he should have been there. He felt very guilty, and entertained the idea of quitting school. An idea he would later give more contemplation.

Soon as Gary got there, Suzie came running out of the house. "I'm so happy you are here." She said, giving him a long tight squeeze. "I haven't heard anything yet."

"Mom, are you okay?" Gary asked, walking her into the house.

Suzie nodded.

"Let's go inside. We'll wait together."

She had the local news on. They were

covering the storm and search efforts. Their family's boat wasn't the only one in trouble or missing. There were two other boats missing and at least one more in trouble.

It took two hours for the first report to come in. "They found a vessel. Everyone is okay." A reporter said. It turned out they were blown way off course, and it had taken them awhile to get their bearings straight.

Gary and Suzie, not getting much information from the news reports, decided to head down to Gracie's Sea Hag, for information and morale support. It was a common meeting place for the town's people. They figured the family from the other fishing boat might be there, and they were right. Everyone from town seemed to be there. A long sea faring tradition was to meet and support each other at Gracie's. It was the glue that held the community together and had been from almost the beginning.

Gary and Suzie were greeted by well-wishers, happy to see them. Everyone was just as worried and distressed as they were. It felt better to be with others, to share the stress and comfort each other.

The news was on. The phone lines were open. They had a scanner programmed to pick up police and Coast Guard reports. It was like being in 'Command Central'.

Finally, after five hours, a new report came in. A boat was found. It began with the scanner. Then the news picked it up. The information was sketchy, at first. The boat had been disabled by the storm. All the people on board were alive. Two. No, three. No, there was a crew of six. It wasn't his family. Gary was very happy they were found, but his anxiety was increasing with every passing hour.

Gary looked over at his Mom. She was exhausted. "Let's get some chowder and go home. We can wait there, and maybe get some sleep." Gary said, taking her hand.

He drove her home. Suzie went into the living room and turned on the television to the local news. Gary went into the kitchen to make some tea and grab some spoons. He brought in the chowder, hoping Suzie would eat something. "Here," Was all he said.

It broke her concentration. She was grateful. The day continued to move along slowly.

Night fell and their fears grew stronger. It's harder to survive on open water after the sun goes down.

In the twilight hours, the call came in. Suzie jumped up, not fully awake. "We found their boat!" Came an official sounding voice, on the other end of the phone. She listened for a while, then hung up.

Gary's Mom turned to him. "They found the boat, capsized. Your Grandfather is okay, but…" Her eyes started tearing up and the words got caught in her throat. "Your Father is still missing." She began crying. Gary just held her as the tears flowed and flowed.

As he stood there comforting his Mother, Gary's thoughts turned to his Grandfather. He would need much care. Suzie could help, but with Mathew missing, it would be a lot for her. Gary decided to take an absence from school, stay to care for his Grandfather and take over the fishing business. Hoping it would all be a temporary situation, Gary told his Mother, "Don't worry. They'll find Dad." He held her tight and said, "I've decided to stay a while and help take care of things."

Suzie looked up at him with a halfhearted

smile. She was hoping he was right about Mathew, but she wasn't sure.

Gary called a neighbor to come and stay with his Mom. Then he rushed out the door to the hospital.

CHAPTER 9

When he arrived the nurse informed him that Bill was okay, but they had him sedated. Gary would not be allowed in to see him until he was awake. He felt good that he was able to be there when he woke up. Gary waited a long time to see his Grandfather. When he realized it would be some time before he was allowed in to see Bill, he decided to call Alice.

"Hi, Alice? Sorry to call so early." Gary said, when he heard a sleepy voice on the other end.

"Hello? Is this Gary?" She asked, wiping the sleep out of her eyes.

"Yes."

"Oh. I heard about your family on the news. I tried to call you."

"Mom and I were at Gracie's."

"I thought you might be. Where are you, now?"

"At the hospital. Waiting to see my Grandfather."

"Did they tell you anything yet?"

"They said he will be okay. He is exhausted and dehydrated. The nurse said I could go in when he wakes up."

"Is there anything I can do?" Alice said, meaningfully.

"No, maybe I could see you later."

"Don't you have to be back in school, Monday?"

"I'm going to take a leave of absence until things are better around here. They really need me."

"I understand." Alice sighed. She knew how hard it would be to get back to school after putting it on hold. She wanted to tell him it was a bad idea, but didn't. It wasn't the time.

"I'll call you later." Gary said. "Thanks."

"For what?"

"For…caring and listening." With that, he

hung up. Just as he was putting the phone down, the nurse came in.

"He's awake. You may see him now."

Gary gathered his coat and followed the nurse.

He entered Bill's hospital room. It was just like he had expected it to be. Bare and sterile. Gary was never sure why, but he always felt a bit nervous visiting someone in a hospital. It wasn't clear to him, but anyone close to Gary, knew it was because it was the last place he saw Jillianne and his child. It was something that he had successfully pushed away. His thoughts only turned to them at certain times of the year, and he had learned to handle those times pretty well.

"Hi, Grandfather." Gary said, walking to Bill's bedside.

He just smiled, a tired smile.

"I came to see how you are doing. Mom is at home, waiting for you."

"Where's my boy? They won't tell me anything." Grandfather said, weakly. He had a lot of concern in his voice.

Gary didn't want to worry or stress him, but decided it was better to be honest. "They haven't found him yet."

Looking down at his blankets, Bill almost cried. After a long silence he asked when he was going to get to leave.

Just then the nurse walked in. "Hi, Mr. Jones. How are you feeling?" She asked, in a cheery voice, as she took his vitals.

"Just fine. When can I leave?" He asked. Bill's voice was weak, but very gruff. He wanted to get back home to find out exactly how the search effort was going.

"The doctor will be in around four o'clock this afternoon. It's two thirty, so it shouldn't be too long." She was smiling a reassuringly, as she said it.

Shortly after the nurse left, Bill turned to Gary. "I don't want to wait 'til four. Let's sneak out?" Gary could see a twinkle in his eye, but knew he was very serious about leaving right then.

"I wish we could, but we need to make sure you are all right first."

"Okay," was all he said. Grandfather was very disappointed.

By four fifteen the doctor hadn't shown, so Gary went to the nurse's station to find out where he was. To his frustration, the doctor had been held up by another patient. The nurse notified him it would be at least another twenty or thirty minutes. Gary went back to his Grandfather's room, to find him getting into his clothes.

"I just want to be ready, when they say I can go." Bill was hoping Gary wouldn't be upset. He was done being cooped up, and far away from the harbor, where he could get the latest information on his boy.

Gary chuckled, shaking his head. His Grandfather still had tenacity.

The doctor walked in. "Hello Mr. Jones. I see you are feeling much better. Are you ready to get out of here?"

"I sure am!" He said, most emphatically.

"Let me have a look at you."

The doctor examined Bill. After a few minutes, he said Bill could go home if, he promised to take it easy for a while. Gary reassured the doctor that he would be well cared for, and out of the hospital they went.

Gary took him to his parents' house to rest. As they drove up, Suzie came out to see if they needed any help. Gary had stopped to buy dinner, and handed it to her. Then he helped his Grandfather out of the car and into the house.

The three of them sat in the living room. "What did the doctor say?" Suzie asked.

"They said, I'm fine." Bill stated. He was tired and grumpy, and very worried.

Suzie looked at Gary. "What did they say?"

Gary smiled. "He'll be fine. They said he should take it easy for a couple of days. It might be good if we stay here, just until the Coast Guard finds Dad." It was the first mention of him since they arrived at the house. Gary knew if his Mother had heard anything she would have told them as soon as they drove up.

"When are you heading back to school?" Bill asked his Grandson. Trying divert their thoughts away from worrying about Mathew.

Gary proceeded to tell him and Suzie his plans for school. They were very unhappy, and tried to talk him out of it. But in the end, his mind was made up. He was staying.

Every day Gary went down to the dry dock. The boat needed a lot of repairs, and it was the only distraction he had. It also kept him close to the local fishing news, and helped him to feel useful. He was there to comfort his Mother and help with the house and his Grandfather's care, but Suzie could handle everything on her own, if she needed to.

Time dragged on. There wasn't any new information for a week. Then the Coast Guard called off the search. They had found the boat and Bill, but nothing else. It looked as though Mathew had perished at sea, but his family never gave up hope.

Gary thought back to when he was a boy. There had been a day that his Father went out to sea, by himself. Bill and Gary were very ill and unable to go out that day. Mathew was overdue and Gary was very worried. His Grandfather sat down with him and told him: "When a Father and Son are close, close as your Father and I are, they always know when the other one needs them. Don't you worry, your Father will be home soon. He is just fine, just a little late."

Two hours later, when Mathew had shown up, coming into the harbor, Bill told his Grandson, "You and your Father are close like he and I are. You will always know when he needs you."

Gary still remembered the warm and happy feeling it gave him, knowing he could trust his feelings and count on the advice of his Grandfather. He knew Bill had been right then, just as he knew his feelings were right, now. They were telling him, his Father was alive and needed him, but he couldn't get anyone to listen. It was very frustrating. Thoughts ran through his mind. He knew if he didn't do anything, he would never see his Father again, and he found himself slipping into a familiar sadness. It was the same feeling he had after losing his wife and child. This time, however, he wasn't willing to allow his depression to overtake him.

About a week and a half after the accident, he had the fishing boat in working order. Gary decided to take it out, telling his Mother he just needed to take a cruise out on the open seas. Bill was healing, and Suzie had everything well in hand. It had only taken him an hour to have the boat loaded and ready to go. Off Gary went, to find his Father and reconcile his feelings of guilt (for going away to school, and not being here the day they set sail).

Even though, Gary had told everyone this trip was just to get away for a bit, his real reason was to find his Father. He couldn't accept that Mathew had drowned. Gary sailed out to the coordinates where they found the boat and Bill. Then he started a grid search, widening it as he went. The sun began to set. Gary found a place to weigh anchor, fixed dinner and turned in for the night. It felt good being back on the water. The rocking of the boat lulled him to sleep.

Sunrise found him up and raring to go. He had eaten breakfast an hour earlier. As soon as he could see, Gary was off to search some more. This went on for the next three days. Up before dawn. Ready to search soon as the sun was up. Rest about noon. Start the search again about thirty minutes later. Then to bed only when it was too dark to see. On the fourth day, around noon, Gary started below to check his supplies, when he noticed something off in the distance. It looked like a large piece of driftwood. He decided to get a closer look. As he drew nearer, it looked different. It was a lot larger than it had originally seemed.

To his amazement, it looked like a dingy. Their small boat they carried on board the fishing boat. Gary sailed in closer. His heart soared. It was a dingy. It was the dingy from their boat! The Coast Guard thought it had broken free and drifted away. He hoped, had been hoping, his Father was able to reach it. Gary knew his Dad was strong and a survivor.

He moved in closer. Soon he was almost close enough to peer over the edge. Gary was scared. He didn't know what he would find. The dingy was just floating. There didn't seem to be any sign of life…Then, he saw something moving. His heart raced! Could it be?! Gary moved in even closer. He reached the dingy and looked inside. Overjoyed and in shock, it was his Father!

Gary quickly tied the dingy off. Then jumped inside to check if his Father was alive. He was! Gary breathed a sigh of relief. His Father was very weak, but conscious.

"Hey, Dad. I'm here. Everything's okay. Let's get you out of here." Gary told his Father as he carried him out of the dingy and into their fishing boat.

Mathew looked up at his son and smiled. He was exhausted. Two weeks at sea with little food and fresh water, left him hungry and dehydrated. Back on the fishing boat, Gary took him below. Gave him a few sips of Gatorade, and tucked him in a bunk. Then went to radio the Coast Guard with his coordinates. A rescue helicopter was dispatched immediately.

After the Coast Guard picked up Mathew, they flew him to the hospital in Newport just twelve miles south of Depoe Bay. Gary was left to take the boat and dingy in. The Coast Guard sent a boat to meet up with him and escort him the rest of the way in. Gary had the Coast Guard contact his Mother and Grandfather.

Suzie put the phone down. "Gary found him! He's alive."

Bill sat nodding. Tears were streaming down his face.

They gathered their things and left the house as quickly as possible. Suzie helped Bill, who was taking a little longer these days, due to the fact he was still recovering. Soon they were out the door. It took them, about fifteen minutes to get to the hospital. Suzie kept finding herself speeding, and slowing down was driving her crazy!

So many thoughts were running through her head. The excitement of seeing her husband alive was making her head spin. When they reached the hospital, Suzie and Bill checked in at the front desk. They found Mathew was already there. The receptionist ushered them to the nurses' station.

"We would like to see Mathew Jones. I am his wife and this is his Father." Suzie said to the nurse on duty.

"I will look him up." She said. The nurse typed something and looked at her screen. "He's in ICU. You may see Mr. Jones as soon as the doctor is done examining him."

"Do you have any information on his condition?" Bill asked.

"The doctor will be out to talk to you before you go back to see Mr. Jones. Would you please wait over there?" The nurse said, as she pointed to a row of chairs in the waiting room. "I'll let you know as soon as the doctor is here." The nurse looked very caring, and shot Suzie a concerned glance.

Suzie and Bill went and sat in the waiting

area. They were very anxious. After twenty minutes went by, the nurse called them. "The doctor will be here shortly."

A minute or two later the doctor appeared in the doorway. "Hello, I am Dr. Edwards." He said, extending his hand to Bill and then to Suzie. "Mr. Jones is in stable condition. He has been through a lot." He said with a rather serious expression. "I expect his stay to last about a week. Right now, he is in Intensive Care, but I am reasonably sure he will be out of there sometime tomorrow."

"Can we see him?" Suzie asked.

"Yes." He answered. Then turned to the nurse sitting at her desk. "Nurse, will please show Mr. and Mrs. Jones to Mathew Jones' room?"

"Thank you, sir." Bill said, shaking the doctor's hand.

Suzie and Grandfather followed the nurse to room 215. "Here it is. Use the nurse call button if you need anything." The nurse said. Then went back down the hall to her desk.

Suzie slowly peeked in the room to see if Mathew was awake. He was sleeping soundly. They went in quietly and sat. About fifteen minutes later, Mathew woke up. Suzie, who had been sitting right next to his bed, reached out her hand and touched his shoulder.

Mathew looked up at her and groggily whispered. "Hi, sweetie."

Suzie smiled. "Your Father is here too. I love you."

Bill walked over to his son's bed. "Hey, son. How are you feeling?"

"Okay." Mathew was very tired. Soon he drifted back to sleep.

"I am going to go see if I can get ahold of Gary. Would you like me to bring something back for you?"

"No, thank you." Suzie answered as he left.

Bill went down the halls of the hospital and found the cafeteria. He got himself a cup of coffee and sat at one of the tables. Sometimes it was easier to rest by himself, especially when he was trying to come down from a stressful time. It was a nice feeling knowing his son was safe and was going to recover.

Soon as he finished his coffee, Bill went and

called Gary. He hoped Gary was close enough to port, so the signal would be strong enough to reach his cellular phone. Otherwise, it would take a little longer, because he couldn't make a direct call to the radio. The phone rang a couple of times. With a lot of crackling, the call got through. "Hello?" Gary answered.

"Hello, Grandson." Bill said through all the static. "I saw your Dad. He's okay. Your Mom is with him. How close are you?"

"I'm just outside the harbor. I'm pulling into Newport. I'll get a taxi and be at the hospital soon. Tell Dad, I love him."

"Okay. See you soon." Bill said as they hung up.

Grandfather headed back to room 215 to see Mathew and Suzie. As he got close to the room, he heard voices. When he entered, he saw Mathew sitting up and talking with Suzie.

"How's my fellow survivor?" Bill said with a grin. "I thought you were a goner." He said gently patting his son's shoulder.

Mathew's face was sun burned and his lips were chapped and scabbed over. It was obvious he had been at the mercy of the elements for a long period of time. He was very tired, but doing much better since being rehydrated. It would take some time, but Mathew would be well soon.

"I spoke to Gary when I went for coffee. He is on his way in, and docking in Newport."

"What?! Why is he out in the boat? Isn't he supposed to be in school?" Mathew didn't remember Gary rescuing him.

"No. He stayed out this semester to be at home and help me with your Father's recovery." Suzie told him. "After the officials gave up hope, he decided to go look for you. He's the one who found you."

"Wow. My son, found me." Mathew said to himself, taking a moment to let it sink in. What a pleasant surprise. A very proud moment for a father.

Mathew's nurse came in, interrupting his thoughts. She introduced herself to everyone in the room. Then took his vitals. "Do you need anything?" She asked Mathew.

"No thank you."

"Okay, then I will be back again in a few hours. Be sure to use your buzzer if you need something." The nurse said as she was leaving.

An hour or so went by. It was very quiet. Mathew was just drifting off to sleep again, and Suzie was thinking about getting a cup of coffee...When she was startled by a knock at the door. It took everyone by surprise.

"Come in." Bill said, while straightening up in his chair.

It was Gary. He was greeted with smiles and winks that said, "He's okay. You did a good job."

"Hi, Dad. How are you feeling?"

"I'm doing pretty well. Thanks to my Son, so I've heard." Mathew flashed a big proud smile at his rescuer.

"I just didn't think you would give up that easily." Gary leaned over and gave his Father a hug. Then he walked over and hugged his Mother and Grandfather.

After a while, Bill asked Gary, "Would you come down to the cafeteria with me. I think we could all use some coffee and sandwiches."

They walked quietly down the corridor. When they got away from the ICU, Bill stopped and spoke to Gary. "You've turned into quite a man." His Grandfather paused, thoughtfully for a moment. "There for a while, I thought we might lose you."

Gary's mind wondered through his memories of being shanghaied.

"But as soon as I met Jillianne and saw how committed you were to each other...I knew we wouldn't." Bill said.

Then Gary realized his Grandfather had been thinking, he was trying to escape family responsibilities, by finding an excuse to stay in New Mexico.

Bill smiled, knowing that what he was saying was sinking in. Then he continued. "A boy grows up, but age isn't the sign of maturity. How you handle what is cast at you, shows where you are in the growing process.

When you were a little boy, I saw a greatness in you. I was worried you would not find it, until late in life. I can see now, that you have found it, whether you realize it or not.

You've survived capture, the loss of your wife and your child. Now, thinking you had lost another loved one, you could have hidden away, consumed yourself with school or fallen into a deep depression. Totally given up. You didn't. Instead you went above and beyond everyone else, and found your Father." He fought back the tears. "I was so afraid I had lost my Son." He paused. Took in a deep breath and slowly exhaled. "Thank you. I am very proud of you." With that Grandfather hugged his Grandson, patted him on the back and off they were to the cafeteria.

Gary didn't know what to say. It didn't seem right to say anything anyway. They just walked on with a better, more mature understanding.

CHAPTER 10

A couple of days later, Mathew was allowed to go home. Allowed being the word. Because he couldn't stand being cooped up any longer. He was just like his Father. They tried to keep him until the end of the week, but Mathew was ready to go. He could be very stubborn. Suzie and the rest of the family knew he would be well cared for at home. With everyone reassuring the doctors, Mathew left the hospital.

They reached home late in the afternoon. Thankfully, Suzie had made a casserole ahead of time and froze it. So she was able to just pop it in the oven, and they had dinner about an hour later. The next day, Gary went to the grocery store and bought everything for a complete chicken dinner. He brought it home and Suzie made an excellent dinner with all the trimmings. Everyone ate better than they had in a long time. It was just the medicine Mathew needed.

As the days passed, Gary could see things were starting to return to normal. He also noticed his bank account was getting lower than he was comfortable with. It was time for him to get a job. It would be months before the next semester of school was to begin.

Gary went down to the docks to see if there was any work. It was difficult. There just didn't seem to be any need for him. Some of the other fishermen offered to take him on, but Gary knew he would be taking money away from their families. Their loyalty to fellow fisherman was commendable, but he couldn't find it in himself to take any of the jobs offered. He ended up working at the local Dairy Queen restaurant. The job only paid minimum wage, but it was steady. Everyone was fun to work with, and it was only temporary, until the next semester started.

During the time he was at home, working and helping is family, he continued to keep in touch with Alice. She had been very concerned about Gary's Father and Grandfather. When he had told her he was going out on the boat, to scout the area where his Father was lost, she was scared, but very supportive. She was the only person he had told why he was really going out on the boat. Although, his Mother had figured it out on her own, before Gary had even left the harbor.

Now that he was staying in town and not

returning to school right away, she was sad. She had hoped he'd be returning soon, to his education. But she had good news, Alice would be back home at the end of the semester. Gary was very happy. He missed Alice. It wasn't until he had been away from her for a while that he realized how much she meant to him.

Time crept by. Alice and Gary talked at least a couple of times a week. When the semester ended, Alice came back as soon as she possibly could. It was a beautiful day. She called his parent's house and found out Gary was at work. As he left the Dairy Queen at the end of his shift, he was surprised to see Alice waiting for him, outside by his car.

Gary walked out the door and almost ran up to her. "I missed you. I'm so happy to see you!" He said, giving Alice a big hug.

"It's good to see you, too!" She said, returning the hug.

"What are you up to?"

"Nothing, I just thought I'd surprise you. I don't have any plans tonight."

"Good. Let's go by Gracie's, grab some

chowder and take it to my parents' house. I told them I'd bring home dinner."

Alice agreed that would be a good idea. She was happy to go along and see Gary's family. It had been a long time since she had seen them.

Suzie was at the door when they came up the walk. "I heard you pull up." She said as she opened the door.

"Look who I found, or should I say, found me." Gary motioned to Alice.

"Hello, Alice. It's so good to see you." Suzie said. "Come on in."

Alice walked through the doorway with Gary following.

Suzie asked Alice, as the three of them walked into the living room. "Are you here on vacation?"

"No. I just finished my last year of teaching. I'm planning on staying here, at least for a little while."

Suzie smiled at her as they entered the living room where Mathew and Grandfather were sitting.

"Hello, Alice." Mathew said standing up to greet her.

Alice could see it was not easy for him to stand. Gary went over to help Mathew. "Dad, it's okay. You don't have to stand. Alice understands." He said.

Alice smiled. "You always make me feel like such a lady, Mr. Jones." She said, referring to the fact that he was always standing to greet ladies. Proper etiquette was important to Mathew. He felt a woman deserved to be shown respect.

Bill smiled. "Hi, Alice. It's good to see you again. How long is your vacation?"

"I'm home, at least for a little while. I completed a year as an art teacher, but I decided to take my career in a different direction."

"Need a job? Want to work on a fishing boat?" Bill grinned, and patted Gary on the shoulder. "Might be fun?"

"Grandpa." Gary said. He was a little embarrassed by his Grandfather's statement, but was happy he approved of Alice.

"We are going to go over to see her family.

They haven't seen her yet. Oh, by the way, we brought you some dinner." Gary said as they began their departing process.

It took about ten minutes to say good-bye. When they were outside, "Your family is so sweet." Alice said, as she took Gary's hand and squeezed it.

Gary smiled.

When they got to her parent's house, Gary walked Alice to the door. They were greeted by her Father. "Hi, sweetheart." He said, giving his daughter a big bear hug.

"Hi, Daddy." She said as she returned his hug. Alice felt squashed and very loved. Her Father had always hugged her that way, being careful not to hurt her.

They walked in the house to say hello to Alice's Mother. After all the hellos, Gary could see Alice's parents and Alice too, wanted some time together to catch up. He made an excuse about being needed at home and having an early day tomorrow. Then said, "Good-bye", to Alice's parents.

Alice walked Gary to the door. When they were out in the hallway, she said, "Thank you," smiled and gave him a peck on the cheek.

Gary smiled and walked out the door. He started home, but decided to go by the harbor to listen to the water flow in and out on the tide. As he sat on the dock he could hear he water slap the underside of where he was sitting. It was a relaxing and comforting feeling to just sit there.

After a couple of hours contemplating his life, Gary decided he'd better get back home. While he was on the docks and all the way home, he thought about his next step in life. Gary was at a cross roads. He could go back to school in the fall as a full time student, finishing his education in three and a half years, or the other options weren't very inviting, if he continued part time it would take him almost seven years to complete, or he could just quit. Quitting was okay, he could follow in his Father's footsteps, taking over the family fishing business. It was a hard rewarding life, and Gary loved being out on the ocean, but he wanted to learn the science of the sea. It was a hard decision. The next few days he spent a lot of time thinking on the subject.

During this time, he found another thing kept creeping into his thoughts. It was Alice. He knew he cared for her, but Gary hadn't expected it to influence him as much as it seemed to be. He tried ignoring his feelings, but it was impossible. In the end, he felt it necessary to recruit Alice, to help him decide.

"You should really consider your educational options." Alice stated, when Gary picked her up for a dinner date. The day before, when he had called to ask her to dinner, he told her about sitting in the harbor the night she got back, and what some of his thoughts had been. "What about going part time?"

"I did think about that, but it would take so long to graduate. I would still be gone three or four days a week. I don't know if it would be worth the crazy schedule. And I'd hoped to be around for my family a little longer." Gary was frustrated.

Alice suggested he call his student advisor at the University. After talking with his advisor, Gary decided to make the long commute every day to and from school. Going to school part-time would push his plans too far back. He wanted to start his future as soon as possible. That meant finishing his degree as soon as possible.

Gary decided to continue with school full time, and stay with Bill. Living at his

Grandfather's, he was able to be around in the evenings when he was needed most. It also gave him time to see Alice a couple of times a week.

She was very happy. Alice had been afraid Gary would have decided to put off going back to school, or would have been stuck at school each semester. All the commuting time concerned her, but she knew he was a confident, capable driver. It felt good knowing he would be close by in the evenings and on the weekends.

School went well for Gary. He thrived. Every day was a new learning experience, so he was never bored. Studying was a joy, because he was truly interested in every subject. It was a memory that he would look back on, fondly.

During his college years, Alice and Gary spent as much time together as they could. First, as old friends, catching up after a long absence. Then, as close companions. Neither one of them were looking for anything more than renewing their friendship, but as time went on they found themselves spending more and more time together. Their friendship slowly blossomed into a casual romance. One day when Gary was walking Alice home, after one of their many evenings together, he stopped her. They were standing atop the sea wall.

The waves were crashing. Just as the sun was disappearing over the horizon, Gary turned and gave Alice a kiss. Feeling his warm gentle lips on hers, she pressed her body closer to his, and returned it with a passion that had been held back for a long time. He let go, and they stood in their embrace, for what seemed like forever, neither one wanting to let go. After their lips parted, they stood there, just holding each other. Soon after, they began walking toward Alice's apartment, in complete, comfortable silence.

From that day forward, their relationship changed. Although, everyone else saw how they felt about each other, long before they did. They both now, knew without a doubt, how the other one felt. Now they were a couple. Closer than they had ever been, even as children.

Gary finally felt comfortable and secure enough to tell Alice about Jillianne and the baby. It was a big step for him. While telling Alice, he found himself reliving all his past emotions, as if the tragedies had happened only yesterday. Difficult as it was, Alice needed to hear about his past. She had heard bits and pieces about Jillianne from different people that knew her, Gary and his family, but she had never heard the complete story.

Alice had known Gary would tell her. When he was ready.

She was very understanding and comforting. Gary was surprised to find out how much it helped him put his past to rest. It was a part of him and always would be, but now he could put his memories away. Where they belonged.

After he passed his third year in college, Gary applied for an internship with NOAA (National Oceanic and Atmospheric Administration). It meant longer hours. He had to complete his final year of college requirements and complete his tasks at work. It was difficult to juggle everything. His new schedule allowed little time for himself, and he still needed to be home at night for his Grandfather. Unfortunately, he had very little time for Alice, but she was very understanding and proud that he was following his dreams.

Gary wanted to marry Alice. He decided he would ask her, hoping to make the engagement a year or two off. One evening, he called Alice. He was very nervous when he asked her to an elegant dinner and an evening of dancing. "It's a celebration." Gary told her, when she asked what the occasion was.

Alice assumed it was to celebrate his internship. She was very excited to spend a special evening with him. At the end of their conversation, Alice was taken by surprised, when he informed her to dress warmly. It was a mysterious request for an elegant evening, and that had made waiting even more exciting.

The next two days were very busy for Gary. He shopped, decorated and ran, what he thought felt like, a million errands. It was a lot of work, but he wanted everything to be perfect.

The day of their date arrived. He drove over to Alice's apartment. Arriving at six o'clock, on the dot. She opened the door to find a very dapper man standing there. He was dressed in a black tux with a black thick over coat.

Alice was in a beautiful tan gunny sack dress. It was loose, but fitted at the shoulders. The dress was a new version of the old classic granny dresses from Gary's Mother's generation. He was happy to see her in something so timeless and with such elegance.

"Come in. I'll be just a minute." She said, motioning to him. Inside she took a long pale blue hooded cape from its hook by the door. "Will you help me with this?"

Of course he obliged. As he draped the cape over her shoulders, "You look absolutely, stunning."

"Why, you don't look so bad yourself." Alice was grinning. Noticeably pleased, with his appearance.

Gary held the door for Alice. She stopped and asked. "So, what restaurant are you taking me to?"

"It's a surprise."

Alice got in the car, full of curiosity. Gary drove toward the harbor. Her mind was racing trying to guess where they were going. The only place in the direction they were headed was a café that the fishermen frequented, but it wasn't elegant. She was confused, until she saw a light coming from Gary's family's boat. Alice smiled. That made Gary very happy.

It was a cool clear evening in September. The moon was full, and there was a light breeze coming off the ocean. Gary parked the car, got out and held the door for Alice, as she departed the vehicle. They walked toward his boat, enjoying the fresh, clean air. As they got nearer, Alice could see the time and care he had put into decorating. The vessel was outlined with rope lights intertwined with fresh roses. The romantic glow was more beautiful than the fanciest candle lit restaurant. They were greeted by soft gentle music, as they approached the deck.

"Ladies first." Gary said, as he held up his hand to help her board the boat. Alice could see a most exquisite table laid out before her. Complete with cloth napkins and crystal glasses. Next, he seated her at the table, holding her chair. "Would you like to start with a glass of wine?"

"Yes, please." Alice was simply glowing. Everything was so beautiful and well thought out.

Gary poured the wine. She could see that he had been taught well, at some point in his life. It was an impressive quality, and surprised her, though she tried not to let it show. "Thank you." She said, as he handed her the glass.

Alice sat sipping her wine. Gary excused himself and went into the galley to do the final preparations for dinner. He was quite comfortable in the kitchen. When he was on his own he had gotten a lot of practice, and found he really enjoyed cooking. As Gary was getting vegetables ready to steam, Alice came in. "I brought you some wine."

"Thank you."

"Looks pretty good." She said, stealing a piece of broccoli. Alice smiled a playful smile, as she stole another piece. Gary pretended to slap her hand away. Alice giggled and gave him a peck on the cheek. It was a cute exchange.

"What am I going to do with you?" He said with a smile.

She shrugged her shoulders. With a grin and a twinkle in her eye, she stole another vegetable and went out to the table.

Gary loved it when she joked. Alice was funny and cute, never carrying a joke too far.

When the food was ready, he brought out their plates. "This looks so good." Alice commented as he served her. There was roast beef, mashed potatoes, gravy and steamed vegetables.

Gary was pleased to see how happy she was. They enjoyed their dinner. When they were finished, Alice helped him take the dishes into the galley. "You sit and relax. This dinner was meant for you. I get to wait on and pamper you." Gary said.

Alice smiled. "I get lonely at the table, all by myself." She pretended to be sad and pouty. Then giggled.

"Okay, you can help." Gary smiled. "Thank you, sweetheart."

The two of them cleared the table, washed the dishes and put the galley in order. Gary poured them another glass of wine. "Let's go sit in the bow."

It was all fixed up with pillows so they could lounge and be comfortable. The rope lights were on the deck, giving just enough of a glow to enhance the mood, but not enough to interrupt their stargazing ability.

Gary sat down and Alice joined him, cuddling up in his arms. "This is wonderful. A perfect evening. I wish it never had to end." She said, happily sighing.

"Does it have to?" Gary said, smiling nervously.

"Of course, silly." She smiled, but then

looked seriously at him. "What do you mean?" She wasn't about to stay the night. It just wasn't her way.

Gary reached behind one of the pillows and pulled out a small gift bag. "I wanted to give you this so many times, but I had to be sure. My feelings have been so unclear to me since I lost Jillianne and the baby. I've felt so very sad and...scared. Sometimes, I thought couldn't face another day. Then you came back into my life. You've always brought out the best in me. You make me happy, especially when nothing else can. I would like you to be with me always." Gary said, as he handed her the bag.

While he was talking Alice had opened her present and found a ring box. As the reality of what he was saying set in, she opened the box. Inside was a modest diamond ring with two small rubies one on each side. It was the most beautiful ring in the world, to Alice. Gary had put so much thought and love into picking it out for her. He even made sure it had rubies, her favorite stone.

Gary took the ring out of the box and held it up to Alice. Taking her left hand, he asked. "Alice would you be my bride?"

Alice was crying happy tears. "Yes. Oh...yes! I will be your bride, and I will try to be the best wife I can."

Gary put the ring on her finger. They sat there for a long time, just holding each other, and watching the stars.

After a while, "I suppose I should take you home." Gary said. "I wish we could stay longer, but I really need to get back to check on my folks."

"I wish we could stay, but it is time we got going." She said with a sigh.

They gathered their things and walked out on the dock. It was such a lovely night and they were so happy. They walked slowly, holding hands in the moonlight, trying to make the evening last just a bit longer.

All the way home and long after, Alice was floating on a cloud. The next evening, she had Gary and his family over for dinner. They announced their engagement. Everyone was very happy. They made a handsome couple, and were so good for each other.

CHAPTER 11

They were married two years later in a ceremony on the shoreline outside Depoe Bay. There were so many people, it seemed as though the whole town had turned out, to see them married. Their lives were busy with school and work, but they managed to take an extra-long weekend, just to themselves. It wasn't much of a honeymoon, but they were just happy to have the time together, without interruptions or responsibilities to anyone but themselves. It was a good start to wonderful life together.

A year after they were married, Gary received a letter. It was from Pedro, the little boy from Mexico that had helped him cross the border back into America. He and Gary had corresponded throughout the years. It had been over a year since he last received a letter from Pedro, and he was very worried about him. Gary had written many times, but his letters were never answered.

In the letter, Pedro explained he would like to come to America, but legally. It was important to him to do things the correct and honest way. There wasn't any work in the town where he lived. He had moved around looking, but the prospects were just as bad in the surrounding areas. Pedro felt the only chance at a future was for him and his Mother to come to America and start a new life. He was writing to find out if Gary would sponsor him.

Gary had a long discussion with Alice and his parents. Everyone was very supportive of helping Pedro, but they left the finale decision up to him. Gary thought long and hard about it. Finally, he spoke to the one person that knew how to help him figure out his own mind, his Grandfather. Bill was fully aware of what would have happened, had it not been for Pedro. He had helped Gary get back into America and that had, most likely, saved his life. Gary decided it was time to return the favor. He wrote to Pedro the next day, to let him know he would sponsor him. Alice had suggested that Pedro come and stay with them until he could get settled in his own place. So it was decided, Pedro would come to Depoe Bay, and stay with them.

Mathew gave him a job working on his fishing boat. Pedro was eager to learn everything he could, and he learned fast. When he got the hang of one thing he would continue with it, and learn everything he could about the job. Once he mastered it, he would find the next thing to master, knowing he could come back to it the next time someone needed the job done. Soon he was helping in almost every aspect of the business. When the off season came, Pedro could be found on the docks helping out where ever he was needed, and learning whatever anyone had time to teach him.

In Mexico, where he had been living, there were very few opportunities for a good job or education. One day, when fishing with Bill, Pedro asked him about learning better English. Bill told him he could take classes at the community college. They had English classes and other learning opportunities he might be interested in. Pedro spoke to Gary about it. When it was time to check it out, Alice took him to see a guidance counselor. He helped Pedro set up a schedule and apply for a student loan. The classes he chose were English as a second language and business management. It was important to him to get a good education. When he wasn't working, he was at the college, doing homework, or reading anything he could get his hands on. He was a very dedicated student.

One evening, when they were all sitting around talking, Pedro opened up about his past. When he was a small boy, he lost his Father. He left for work, one morning, and never returned. Pedro had known that his Father had been working with the coyotes, smuggling people across the border. His Mother told him the other competitors decided they wanted to extend their territory and his Father had just gotten in the way of a stray bullet. It was wrong for him to smuggle people, and Pedro knew it. His Father felt pushed into a corner. He couldn't find work, and with a wife and child to care for, Pedro's Father didn't see any other way to keep his family fed and a roof over them. His Father and Mother had always taught him to be a good boy. They didn't want to see him mixed up in anything illegal. After his Father died, Pedro and his Mother sold what they could to buy food to make tamales to sell. Their little Tamales business was enough to keep them fed and housed, most of the time.

Then, one day, Pedro met Gary. After seeing how badly Gary wanted to get home to America, Pedro started thinking how much better it might be there. He had seen all the people from his country, that tried to cross the border, but he wasn't sure if what they were looking for really existed. So Pedro decided to write to the address Gary had given him. It was his home address in Depoe Bay, so it had taken some time for Gary to receive it and write back. In the letter, Pedro asked a lot of questions about what it was like to live in America. Gary had answered as best he could. At that point in his life, he was just trying to figure out what life was all about for himself, but he was able to tell Pedro a lot about America. He learned a lot through Gary's letters to. It took him many years to decide to take a risk, and try moving to a new country. Shortly after coming to America, he never looked back.

Now that he was in America and working, he sent some of his money to his Mother. He kept some to pay his expenses, and the rest he put away to bring his Mother home to live with him. What he made working wasn't enough to get his Mother home very quickly, so Pedro did many things on the side. He repaired nets, and when someone needed a hand, he was the first to volunteer. The fisherman had a great respect for him and his work ethic.

Pedro lived with Gary and Alice for almost five years. During that time Alice gave birth to twins, a boy and a girl. They named the boy William, after Gary's Grandfather, and the girl Ellie, because it had always been Alice's favorite name for a girl. Gary was so proud, but it was a very difficult time for him. When he found out Alice was pregnant, things came rushing back to him. He was afraid, all throughout her pregnancy. It was hard for Alice.

She tried to comfort Gary, explaining very few pregnancies have such severe complications. Especially, ones resulting in the death of the mother or the child. Her assurances failed to ease Gary's fears. He was nervous all the time, and it was effecting Alice. The stress was bad for her.

Pedro spoke to Mathew one day while they were out at sea. He told Mathew how nervous and scared Gary was, and how it seemed to be effecting Alice. Mathew thanked Pedro. Later, Mathew spoke to Gary. They had a good long talk. Gary had not noticed how much his emotions showed. He worked very hard at keeping his feelings of apprehension to himself. When things began to get difficult for him, Gary decided to go to his Father or Grandfather and talk his feelings out. It helped keep him sane. Alice was able to relax and concentrate on taking care of herself and the unborn twins. She and Gary were grateful to his family, for all their emotional support, and especially to Pedro, for speaking up.

After the babies were born, Gary was a lot more at ease. Even during Alice's second pregnancy, he was a lot more relaxed. They had another boy, and named him Joseph. Then, they decided, it was time to stop having children. Alice wanted to go back to teaching art, and Gary was very busy with his work. She found teaching rewarding and wanted to continue when the children were old enough to start school.

When the twins were four years old and the youngest boy was three, Alice began teaching an art class for preschoolers at the local community center. It began as a way she could teach and share her passion for art with her children. Suzie came along and helped keep an eye on all three children, while Alice was teaching the class. Alice found working with the children was much different than she had expected it to be. She enjoyed the way the children took to each project. They were able to be completely open and uninfluenced by anyone. All their ideas were original. The classes became a free flowing river of inspiration and creativity. With adults their creativity was all dammed up. Each part of the dam represented a time in their life when they felt a failure in their artwork. It was very refreshing to come to class each day, and know that something new and interesting was waiting for her. She had seen it every day at home, with her own children, but never realized how much it could energize her life until, she was completely immersed in it.

In the summer following, Pedro came to Gary, he had some good news. He had saved enough money to start the process of bringing his Mother to America. Gary and Alice had asked him to stay, until he had enough money for a good start, and for the cost of getting his Mother here. He had, and now he was ready to move on, with his finances in order, he started looking for an apartment.

It was a very wonderful time for Pedro. He had never had a place of his own. There were so many things for him to do. Mathew went with Pedro to look at different apartments. When he found the one he wanted, Mathew went, but stayed out of the renting process. Pedro had learned many things since coming to America. He always did his research and got advice from Gary and his family. The paperwork went smoothly, and soon, Pedro was moving in.

A month went by. Pedro saw or spoke very little to his friends. Gary was a somewhat concerned, but knew he had a lot going on. One afternoon, Suzie got a phone call, Pedro invited Gary, Alice, Bill, Mathew, Suzie and of course, the three children to dinner at his new place. She passed the message on to the rest of the family. Everyone accepted the invitation and were very excited. The apartment was in perfect order. The décor was simple and masculine, perfect for a young man starting out on his own.

It took Pedro six months to get the paperwork together, and get his Mother to America on a temporary visa. After that, Pedro and his Mother worked with immigration, so she could stay and become a citizen. Pedro had been working on his for a long time, and was about to take his citizenship test. He was happy his Mother was there when he took the test. When he passed, she was able watch him take the oath. They were both very proud.

His Mother became a citizen about three years after coming to America. There was a lot to do, but when it was all done, she was a citizen. She and Pedro were very happy living in Depoe Bay. Pedro supported his Mother and she was able to retire in comfort. Every day she would walk down to the sea wall and look out over the ocean. It was so peaceful. She had not had much peace throughout her life. Pedro's Mother was very happy.

CHAPTER 12

After giving birth to their three children, they decided to adopt. It started out with one foster child that had started coming to the community center art classes. The little girl's parents had died in an automobile accident, when she was three. She was very lonely, and in need of a family. Alice took to her right away. She and Gary decided to become foster parents, and fell in love with her. They filed the adoption papers. The process took a long time, but they were approved.

One evening Gary came to Alice. Knowing how much she enjoyed teaching the children, he asked her if she wanted to stay teaching. She thought about it. Alice decided it was more rewarding to teach, and raise children than to have a career working with adults in stuffy art galleries. She was not making much money, but she was happy. Besides, Gary's job paid more than enough to cover the bills. They decided Alice would stay teaching at the community center, indefinitely.

Their decision changed their lives more than they expected. The social worker that helped them with their adoption kept their name on file. When a child about three or four needed a foster family he called Gary and Alice. They only refused a few. Fostering children for a short time was okay, until they started getting attached to each child. Gary and Alice adopted five more before they reluctantly decided to stop adopting and fostering. It was getting difficult to keep up with all of them, and Gary and Alice were getting older. They wanted to enjoy their children, not feel burdened by over committing themselves, to too many.

Gary and Alice were wonderful parents. Gary taught his children to be self-reliant, respectful and most importantly, to be themselves. Alice taught them to discover their talents. She encouraged them to express themselves and make the most out of life. Their home was a happy one, always buzzing with activity.

Bill lived to be a hundred and two. After Gary and Alice were married, he moved in with Mathew and Suzie. They took care of him until he passed away. It was Bill's wish to never have to live in a care home, and he never had to, because they were able to have in home care three times a week. Grandfather loved and was proud of all his grandchildren. Staying true to his story teller spirit, he continued to tell salty stories of the sea, Depoe Bay and the surrounding areas. His grandchildren continue to pass his stories on.

Mathew continued to fish until he was well into his seventies. When he decided to retire, Gary and his Father decided to keep the boat. Pedro continues the fishing tradition and runs the business. He turned out to be a very good and fair business man. As Gary's children grew, some of them joined the business, working under Pedro. The business continues to be owned by the Jones' family.

Mathew and Suzie made wonderful grandparents. Mathew lived to ninety-nine and Suzie lived to be ninety-five. They saw all of their grandchildren and most of their great-grandchildren come into this world and start their lives. When Suzie passed away it was her time. She died peacefully, at home. Mathew's health had been declining for years, and six months after Suzie, he passed on to heaven to be with his sweetheart.

Suzie was the glue that kept everything together. During all the trials of Gary's life, he always knew he could turn to her. She was quiet, supportive and slow to judge. If she felt there was something she needed to correct, she had a way of doing it, so that the person being corrected wasn't even aware that it was her idea to change their path. She had a kind of quiet wisdom that she was able to pass down to Alice. It was something Alice was grateful for, and passed on to her children.

William, Ellie and Joseph, as well as the six children Gary and Alice adopted, grew into strong, self-reliant individuals. Bill, Mathew and Gary started them out early, sharing the family's fishing traditions with them.

All of the children loved to fish. Most of them continued with the family business. Ellie and Joseph were the exceptions. They followed in Alice's footsteps. Just as their Father was happy and freest on the open ocean, they, like their Mother, were happiest in an art studio, creating.

For a life that started out turbulent and full of uncertainty, Gary's had turned out exceptional. He made it through all the tragedy, sometimes barely, but when he looked back on his life, he smiled. So much had happened. He came from a small town, saw and did things most young men, only imagined. He had two great loves, and was able to share his stories and lessons with of all his children. It was an adventuresome life. He felt blessed, and was never bored.

ABOUT THE AUTHOR

Patricia Thompson (1973-) is a devoted mother of three independent teenage girls, and wife of a retired member of Search and Rescue. She grew up in Portland, Oregon and spent many summer vacations on the Oregon Coast. She enjoys teaching, writing and caring for her family.